Raven's Wharf

A.B. Martin

For Beatrice
With all my love

Chapter One

Captain Parker inhaled sharply, his eyes widening with alarm. This was way beyond anything he had faced in his twenty years of flying, and he had no idea how he was going to deal with it. It was as if the autopilot had seized control of the plane and, whatever he tried, he couldn't get it back under his command.

'What's going on?' he said, his eyes darting around the instrument panel. 'Why aren't the controls responding?'

The co-pilot stared blankly back at him, a look of blind terror on his face. He was an inexperienced rookie who had only been with the company for a few months. Parker knew he would have to deal with this on his own.

As he continued to run through the controls, desperately searching for a solution, small beads of sweat began to form on his forehead and the muscles in his neck and shoulders became rigid and tight. There was no margin for error. Get this wrong, and he was facing a major catastrophe. The plane was hurtling along at thirty thousand feet, and Parker had no idea how he was going to bring it safely back to the ground.

'Spooky, isn't it?' said a voice in his earpiece. It was the voice of a young woman, and she sounded like she was enjoying Parker's discomfort. He straightened up and looked all around, wondering where the voice might have come from.

'Don't worry, Captain,' the young woman continued. 'I've got control of the plane now. I'm just going to fly it around for a while and see what this metal tube can do.'

'Who is this?' Parker shouted. 'And what on earth do you think you're playing at?'

There was no response from the young woman.

'I said, who is this?' he shouted again. 'I demand you hand back control of my aircraft!'

'Relax, Captain,' said the young woman. 'We're only having a bit of fun. You sit back and put your feet up. I'll take it from here.'

The captain and co-pilot looked at one another with an increasing sense of dread. They had no idea who this woman was, but one thing was certain. They were now facing a full-scale emergency.

'Whatever happens, we have to keep this from the passengers,' said Parker. 'The last thing we need here is mass panic.'

Back in the passenger section of the plane, Mrs Watson was blissfully unaware of the drama that was playing out in the cockpit. She was nearly home. Her husband and daughter were waiting for her at the airport, and she was looking forward to seeing them again and enjoying a well-earned evening of relaxation.

She leaned back and closed her eyes as the cabin crew ran through the landing procedure. The more experienced members of the crew must have done this a thousand times, yet they still managed to sound enthusiastic and committed. Headrest in the upright position, seat belt on, it was the usual stuff. Mrs Watson had heard it so many times before.

The next announcement was a bit of a shock. The pre-announcement chimes sounded, but instead of being followed by the captain speaking the passengers heard the voice of a young woman.

'Hello everyone,' she said. 'I hope you're having a great flight. Make sure your seat belts are buckled up real tight now, we're going to give the folks on the ground a bit of an air show.'

The cabin crew looked at one another in surprise and concern. Who was this woman? And what was she talking about? They were even more alarmed when, a few seconds later, the co-pilot burst from the cockpit and moved quickly down the aisle towards the chief flight attendant. He hustled her into the galley, and they spoke in urgent whispers.

'Last chance to strap yourself in,' said the young woman. 'You people are about to experience the thrill of a lifetime.'

A frisson of tension ran through the aircraft. What was going on? Why did the cabin crew look so panicked? Mrs Watson sat bolt upright and gripped the armrests of her seat. She didn't want the thrill of a lifetime. She just wanted to get safely back to her family.

On the main concourse of the airport terminal, twelve-year-old Sophie Watson stared up at the arrivals board, searching for flight UK417. So far, everything seemed to be going to plan. Only twelve more minutes and her mum's plane should be safely back on the ground.

She thumbed in a text to her dad to give him an update. Having dropped Sophie and her friend Sienna at the airport entrance a few minutes earlier, he had driven off to find somewhere to park the car.

'Mum's plane's on time,' the text read. 'We're in the coffeehouse opposite the arrivals board.' It was followed by three thumbs up emojis.

'Brilliant,' he texted back. 'With any luck, we'll be home in time to watch the football.'

Thirty thousand feet above them, Mrs Watson wasn't feeling quite so confident. Something was wrong; she could sense it. She looked out of the window at the frozen fields of Surrey and the tiny cars that were buzzing along the minuscule, well-defined roads. It all looked so safe down there, predictable, secure and free from danger. Biting her lip, she looked around at the other passengers. The happy chat was over. The whole plane was now gripped by a rising sense of terror.

To confirm their worst fears, the plane rocked suddenly as if it had been buffeted by a strong wind, then it banked hard to the left and started descending sharply. As the passengers let out shrieks of panic, Mrs Watson stiffened and looked out of the window once again. Now she was convinced there was a problem. They were approaching the ground a lot faster than normal, and the cabin crew were starting to look as terrified as the passengers.

Back at the airport, the arrivals board was suddenly a mass of confusion. Information was changing every few seconds. Everything had been thrown into a complete meltdown. Two minutes ago the system seemed to be working normally, but now it was a raft of delayed and diverted flights.

Sophie and Sienna walked across to the vast panoramic window that gave a view of the runway. In the distance, they could see a plane behaving erratically and descending at quite a speed. It was rocking slightly as if the pilot didn't quite have it under control, and it didn't look like it was heading for either of the runways.

On board the plane, Captain Parker was still desperately trying to regain control of his aircraft. He tried to make contact with air traffic control, to alert them to what was going on. Halfway through his opening sentence, he was interrupted by the young woman's voice.

'Sorry, Captain, I've still got control of communications,' she said, mocking his mounting distress. 'I'll give you your plane back once we've shown the folks on the ground what this thing can do.'

'Who is this?' Parker shouted, boiling over in frustration. 'There are one hundred and fifty-seven passengers on board this aircraft and your selfishness and stupidity is going to kill us all!'

But there was no response. The girl had gone.

Parker looked out of the front window of the cockpit. He was an experienced airman who had been flying for many years, and he could tell they were approaching the ground at far too great a speed. In the distance, he could see the airport and the motorway beyond it filled with traffic. He knew that if anything went wrong, it wouldn't just be the lives of those on board that would be lost. It could also wipe out hundreds of innocent people on the ground. He had to find a way to regain control, or this could be an absolute catastrophe.

A host of anxious thoughts were rushing through Mrs Watson's head. Had someone broken into the cockpit and taken over the plane? Were there terrorists on board? She thought about her husband and her daughter Sophie, waiting for her at the airport, and she wondered whether she would ever see them again.

All around her, the other passengers were in a state of panic. A man in the seat in front of her was openly sobbing. Others were wide-eyed and grim-faced, saying nothing. A man in a dark blue suit leapt to his feet and started remonstrating with the chief flight attendant, demanding to be told what was going on. She pleaded with him to sit down and put his seat belt back on, but he had lost control and become a little hysterical.

By now, it was obvious to everyone in the airport that there was a major problem. They crowded against the panoramic window and looked up to the sky, praying that their friends and loved ones were safe. Only one plane was visible but, rather than heading towards either of the runways, it looked like it might fly straight past the airport building. Even from this distance, Sophie could see that it bore the famous colours of UK Airlines. It was her mum's plane. She knew it. She put her hand to her mouth and stared at the sky in shock.

This was now developing into a full-scale emergency. Fire crews had been mobilised. They streamed out onto the tarmac, their sirens blaring and lights flashing. Air traffic control had cleared the skies, and all other aircraft had been diverted from the area. For several minutes they had been desperately trying to make contact with the pilot, but they were getting no response.

The plane was still descending at a rapid rate. Captain Parker knew that the landing gear should have been lowered by now, but there was nothing he could do. Someone else had control of the aircraft, and there was no telling what her next move would be.

They were now so close to the airport that Sophie could hear the roar of the plane's massive engines. It tipped its wing to one side, banked hard to the right and started heading back towards the airport building. Sophie gasped in horror at the recklessness of such a move.

Inside the plane, the terrified passengers screamed out in panic as hand luggage tumbled out of the overhead lockers. Everyone was now seated. Even the man who had been remonstrating had buckled up his seat belt and was sitting ashen-faced, staring at the seat in front of him.

They were now only about two hundred feet above the ground, still moving at tremendous speed in the direction of the airport building. It looked like the plane was going to fly right past the panoramic window like the star attraction at an annual air show. It was a massive A320 airbus built to carry almost two hundred passengers, and the pilot seemed to be flying it around for fun.

Sophie stared up at the sky, unable to believe that this colossal beast was travelling so fast so close to the ground. This was insane. It was every passenger's worst nightmare, and Sophie was living each second as if she was there on the plane with her mum. Sienna reached out a comforting arm, aware of the torment that Sophie was going through. All they could do was stand and watch as the massive aircraft flashed past the airport building then slowly started to climb back up into the sky.

It was a steep ascent. On board the aircraft several people were praying and a young flight attendant was weeping uncontrollably, believing she was about to die. Mrs Watson sat staring straight ahead, fearing the worst but clinging to any glimmer of hope. While the terrified passengers wondered what they would be faced with next, the young woman's voice came through on the communication system once again.

'Yee-haw,' she shouted. 'That was better than any fairground ride.'

The plane continued to ascend steeply, taking it away from the chaos of activity on the ground. Then it circled around and repeated the flypast as if a small child was playing with a little toy. Screams of terror accompanied every movement of the plane. To the passengers, it felt like they were riding on the most horrendous roller-coaster they could imagine. The plane dropped into another hair-raising dive, flashed past the airport building, then slowly started to climb back up again. It was a massive relief to see the tarmac moving further and further away from them. They were still alive. There was still hope. Eventually, Captain Parker heard the young woman's voice again, and this time she sounded a little delirious.

'OK, Captain, you can have your plane back now,' she said. 'Thanks for playing with me.'

Parker grabbed hold of the controls and was relieved to discover that they were finally responding to him.

'I don't know who you are,' he shouted. 'But whoever you are, you're in big trouble.'

'Yeah, right,' said the young woman, laughing dismissively. 'As you said Captain, you don't know who I am. So how much trouble can I be in?'

Captain Parker didn't respond. He had more urgent matters to deal with. He guided the plane up to a safe altitude then turned on the onboard communication system.

'Chief Flight Attendant, please report to the cockpit. I'm taking us up to five thousand feet and requesting urgent permission to land.'

The passengers held their collective breath. Could this nightmare finally be over? Whatever madness they had been caught up in, Mrs Watson was beginning to believe that the danger had now passed. But what had it all been for? And more importantly, who was that young woman?

Chapter Two

Sienna wasn't like the other girls that Sophie knew. For one thing, she wasn't from this world. She was from a different world in a different universe.

Sophie didn't like to refer to her friend as an alien. It conjured up images of eerie creatures emerging from UFOs to try to take over the earth, and Sienna was nothing like that. But there was no doubt that she was an extraterrestrial.

She looked just like any of Sophie's other friends as they wandered around the streets of Hampton Spa together. And when she spoke, she sounded just like them as well. She had a microchip implanted in her brain that gave her the ability to speak and understand the local language. It meant she could move around freely, and nobody had the slightest idea where she was really from.

Sienna burst into Sophie's life halfway through the summer, having travelled through a portal from a parallel world called Galacdros. At sixteen years of age, she was the youngest member of a security force called The Elite, and she was searching for Osorio, a fugitive who had stolen a precious artefact called The Orb of Nendaro. Sienna had been charged with recovering The Orb and returning it to its rightful place in the Galacdros Senate and, despite her youth, she was determined to track Osorio down and complete her mission.

At first, Sophie didn't know what to make of her. Sienna was daring and courageous and unflinching in the face of adversity. She was a risk taker who was always keen to meet a challenge head-on. Sophie was nothing like that. She lived a much more sedate life in the affluent Kentish town of Hampton Spa. In fact, the lives the two girls were living couldn't have been more different. But sometimes people just click, despite their differences, and Sophie and Sienna quickly became very good friends.

Life with Sienna was never dull. In the five months the girls had known one another, Sophie had been drawn into a series of terrifying adventures as Sienna sought to complete her mission. First on mysterious

Kestrel Island, where they were hunted down and shot at like wild animals, and then in the murky world under Crook's Wood on the outskirts of Hampton Spa. It was a nightmarish experience and both the girls were lucky to be alive.

When Sophie thwarted Osorio's plot to assassinate the British Prime Minister, she was attacked by his armed guards in her own home. Miraculously, the girls survived this confrontation with his evil cohorts, but Sienna was still without The Orb and Osorio was still at large.

It was now mid-December, and there had been no sightings of Osorio since their last encounter in Crook's Wood in late October. Sienna needed some kind of breakthrough. She contacted Jutan, a senior Galacdros agent now living in this world, and asked if she could meet the girls in Hampton Spa.

'What did she say?' Sophie asked, once Sienna had finished the call.

'She said she'd meet us at the café in Market Square at 10.30. That just gives me time to deal with those emails your mum asked me to send out this morning.'

Sienna was now working for Sophie's mum on a part-time basis, carrying out minor clerical duties in her

Hampton Spa office. Since becoming the Member of Parliament for Hampton Spa, Mrs Watson's workload had increased enormously. And as the Watsons were letting Sienna stay at their house for the foreseeable future, she was keen to help out wherever she could.

'You know, for a security officer, you make a pretty good P.A.' said Sophie, good-naturedly mocking her friend.

'I don't know what that means,' said Sienna, smiling back at her, 'but I'm assuming P.A. stands for pretty awesome.'

Spits and spots of rain were starting to fall as the girls trudged through the frozen streets towards the town. It was a day for thick jackets, scarves and gloves. On reaching Market Square, they dodged their way through the bustling crowds of Christmas shoppers to the little café at the other side of the market.

It was mid-morning, and the café was buzzing with activity. Young mothers sat and chatted together, some with toddlers struggling in their laps, while office workers queued for take-away coffees in an effort to break up the monotony of their morning. It was a hearty and good-tempered atmosphere. The market traders who had made the café their home were bantering good-naturedly with one another, welcoming every familiar face who came through the door.

'Grab that table over there,' said Sophie, pointing to a spot at the far side. 'I'll go up and order some drinks.'

They had only been in the café for a few minutes when the door opened, and an elderly lady entered. She was a tall woman with a dignified air, and she wore a beautifully tailored coat and an elegant hat with a feather attached with a hatpin. She looked a little out of place in the earthy market café, but she had such an air of confidence about her that nobody gave her a second look. When she saw the girls had already arrived, she smiled and strode purposefully over to the table to join them.

'Hello ladies,' she said, pulling out a chair and sitting down. 'I trust I find you both in good health.'

'Hello Jutan,' said Sienna. 'Thank you for agreeing to meet us.'

Jutan was a former head of The Elite in Galacdros and had once been Sienna's father's commanding officer. Having retired from The Elite several years ago, she had now taken up a position on earth, liaising between the security forces in both worlds. Sienna valued her wisdom and experience more than anyone she had ever met, and she often called on her if she felt in need of a little guidance.

Despite the hustle-bustle of the café, Jutan quickly caught the eye of the woman working behind the counter. She nodded at her and smiled, and the woman got to work immediately, appearing to know exactly what Jutan wanted.

'I heard about what happened at the airport on Saturday,' said Jutan, looking thoughtfully at Sophie. 'It must have been a heart-stopping experience knowing that your mother might be on that aircraft.'

'It was horrible,' said Sophie, shuddering at the memory of it. 'At one point, I thought the plane was going to crash right through the observation window. What on earth was the pilot thinking of?'

'Well,' said Jutan, 'when the police interviewed the pilot, he claimed that someone had hacked into the onboard computer system and taken control of the aircraft. And the co-pilot has corroborated his story.'

'Someone hacked into the computer system?' said Sienna. 'How could they? Were they already on the plane?'

'I don't think so,' said Jutan. 'British security services think that someone on the ground may have accessed the controls remotely and overridden the security measures that are in place.'

'But how is that even possible?' Sophie asked.

Despite being only twelve years old, Sophie was a bit of a computer geek. She had been obsessed with coding for as long as she could remember, and she had learned a tremendous amount from her web designer father.

'I don't know how they managed to do it,' Jutan answered, 'but whoever did this is operating at the very edge of our current knowledge.'

'So do you think it was terrorists?' Sienna asked.

'Well, we've been right through all the CCTV footage from the surrounding area and, at the time of the incident, there was a car parked just outside the perimeter fence with two people sitting in it. One of them was a girl about your age Sienna, and the other was a tall man with a dark goatee beard.'

'Osorio!' said Sienna, her eyes widening with excitement.

'Yes, I'm afraid so,' said Jutan. 'It does look a lot like our friend Osorio.'

They stopped talking for a moment when the woman behind the counter arrived with Jutan's coffee. It was her usual drink, a double espresso with a small glass of water.

'Thank you,' said Jutan.

When the woman left, Sienna looked at Jutan quizzically.

'Do you come into this café a lot?' she asked.

'No, it's the first time I've ever been here. Charming little place though.'

'Then how did she know what to bring you?' Sophie asked.

'Lucky guess, I suppose,' said Jutan, smiling radiantly.

Sienna knew that this wasn't the case. The people of Galacdros are experts at mind reading and thought transference, and Jutan had obviously planted the thought in the woman's mind. She may have had a clear memory of Jutan walking up to the counter to order her drinks, but the girls knew that it never actually happened. Sienna was impressed by Jutan's level of expertise.

'But what possible motive could Osorio have for taking control of that plane?' said Sophie, keen to know more about what had happened to her mum.

'I don't know,' Jutan answered. 'We're also very interested in who that girl was. British security services couldn't identify her, so I've sent the footage back to our people in Galacdros. I'm waiting to hear if there's anything about her on their records.'

'Do you have any thoughts on who she might be?' Sienna asked.

'Nothing concrete,' said Jutan, 'but I do have a

hunch. A few weeks ago someone hacked into the central computer at the Senate building in Galacdros, stole a lot of sensitive information and published it online. The files they hacked into were completely wiped but for a message that read "You have just had a visit from Nightfly." My concern is that these two computer hacks may have been carried out by the same person.'

'Nightfly?' said Sienna, 'I've heard that name before somewhere.'

'Yes. It's the codename of a notorious computer hacker on Galacdros. There have been several serious computer hacks on the Senate over the last year or so, and in all of them investigators have discovered that same message.'

'And now you think Nightfly could be working with Osorio, is that it?' said Sophie.

'That is my fear,' said Jutan. 'If Osorio has teamed up with a hacker who has that level of ability, no computer on earth will be safe.'

'I wonder what they're up to,' said Sienna. 'Osorio wouldn't have taken over that plane just for fun. I can't imagine him doing anything for fun. So what else is he planning?'

'Well, that's what we have to find out,' Jutan answered.

Sienna furrowed her brow and looked intently across the table at Jutan.

'What happened to Osorio? He used to be such a good friend to my father. They had big dreams and were so idealistic about the future. Now he regards my father as his mortal enemy.'

'Osorio became obsessed by power,' Jutan replied. 'As he grew in stature inside the Senate, he believed he was the only person who was bold enough to lead our people. He wanted us to invade and colonise other worlds so we could build an empire that our people would be proud of. But your father had seen enough of war. He was intent on leading our people to a peaceful future.'

'But Osorio must realise that eventually he will be brought to justice?'

'Maybe not,' said Jutan. 'What makes him such a difficult opponent is that he thinks he has right on his side. He looks upon himself as a principled warrior who is standing up to the complacent and self-interested state. He believes that he is the hero in this story.'

The idea of Osorio ever being considered a hero was preposterous to Sienna. She had watched her father's devotion to the people of Galacdros and the selfless way he had given service, both as a highly decorated officer in The Elite and as a well-respected senator. In Sienna's eyes, Osorio was an outcast, a fugitive who had committed crimes against her people.

'I take it you've had no sightings of him since your last encounter in October?' Jutan asked.

'No, he seems to have completely disappeared,' Sienna answered. 'I was hoping you might have some information I could follow up on.'

'I thought that might be the case,' said Jutan, 'so I made a few enquiries before I left this morning. The security services think he may be staying at one of the properties owned by the businessman James Masterson, and I've drawn up a list of possible locations. But if you decide to investigate any of them, do so with great care. Masterson is a ruthless man who won't take kindly to anyone poking their nose into his affairs.'

British security agents were convinced that James Masterson was the driving force behind a secret society that was intent on seizing power across the globe. Osorio was thought to be part of the group, and Jutan believed it also included the British Home Secretary Harry Jacobs.

She handed a sheet of paper to Sienna. It was a list of

addresses that had been handwritten in Jutan's elegant handwriting. Sienna studied it for a moment, but her knowledge of the local area was fairly limited, so she handed the list across to Sophie.

'Some of these are quite a way out,' said Sophie 'but this Oak Green address isn't that far. Maybe we could take a look at it this afternoon?'

'Excellent,' said Jutan. 'Let me know if you come up with anything. I'll be in town for the next couple of days, and then I have to go to London for a while.'

'Oh, really?' said Sophie, smiling across at her. 'We'll be in London this week as well. The Prime Minister has invited me to have afternoon tea at Downing Street on Friday, so my parents are treating us to a few days in a nice London hotel.'

'How wonderful,' said Jutan. 'And tea at Downing Street is the least the Prime Minister should do for you. If you hadn't thwarted that assassination attempt when he was here in October, he might never have made it out of this town alive.'

'I'm sure his security people would have stopped the assassin if I hadn't got there in time,' said Sophie.

'Well, that's decent of you to say so,' said Jutan, 'but if the security people had suspected for one moment that the Prime Minister's life was at risk that gunman would never have been able to get as close as he did.'

'Jutan's right,' said Sienna. 'If you hadn't launched yourself at that assassin, he would have had a clear shot at the Prime Minister.'

'Precisely,' Jutan added, 'and your invitation to Downing Street is very well deserved.'

Sophie smiled and averted her gaze. She still hadn't become accustomed to being in the limelight, and she found it difficult to see herself as a hero. She picked up the list of addresses again and tried to move the conversation on to a different subject.

'So we'll have a look at this address in Oak Green,' she said, 'and maybe we could check out one or two of the London properties while we're there this week.'

'Splendid,' said Jutan. 'But make sure you stay alert while you're in London. When you foiled that assassination attempt, you made enemies of some very powerful people. And if they were prepared to kill the Prime Minister, they would think nothing of doing the same to both of you.'

Sophie didn't need to be told. Ever since Osorio's guards had tried to attack her in her own home, she knew that her life would never be the same again. She was in this with Sienna until the bitter end. They would either have to defeat Osorio and reclaim The Orb or she would be forever looking over her shoulder.

Chapter Three

Despite the dark clouds that were mustering on the horizon, it was still dry when the girls left the house and walked the short distance to the bus stop. Sophie was sure that the journey wouldn't take too long. It was only a short ride to their hopping off point on the outskirts of Oak Green, but that didn't take into account the haphazard timetable of the local bus company. It was twenty minutes before the bus finally arrived and by that time the overhead clouds were heavy and charcoal grey, making it dark enough for the bus's headlights to be on.

When they finally reached their destination, they were out in the open countryside. In the gathering gloom, Sophie paused for a moment in an effort to get her bearings. The house they were looking for was an isolated cottage that was last known to be occupied by a tenant farmer. She took out her phone and punched the address into Google Maps.

'It looks like it's down that road over there,' she said, pointing to a small one-track road bordered by hedges.

'Wow,' said Sienna. 'If Osorio really is out here, he couldn't have picked a more remote location.'

'Maybe he's decided to turn over a new leaf and spend the rest of his days farming turnips,' said Sophie, looking to keep the mood light-hearted.

Sienna shook her head and gave her a wry smile.

They moved cautiously down the narrow road, keeping a watchful eye out for vehicles coming from either direction. This was the heart of the countryside. In small communities, people notice things that are not part of their normal experience. They ask questions if they see someone they don't recognise, so the girls were keen to keep themselves well hidden. If they heard anyone coming, they intended to duck into the tall hedge that grew up along either side of the road. It was lush and overgrown, and they were certain it would provide enough protection. But they needn't have worried. Nobody and nothing passed them in either direction.

After walking for about half a mile, they caught a glimpse of a thatched roof a little further down.

'There it is,' said Sienna, her eyes widening with

excitement. 'Let's move down to those trees so we can get a better look at it.'

In the gathering winter gloom, the dark grey sky felt like it was bearing down on them. Sophie was sure they were about to be caught up in a torrential downpour. She pulled up the hood of her waterproof jacket as the first few spots of rain pattered against the ground.

Crouching down behind a large willow tree that towered over the garden, they watched the cottage for a few minutes. It was surprisingly well maintained for a property that had occupied the same land for hundreds of years. At first glance, there seemed to be someone living there. There was a car parked at the side of the house, and a thin wisp of smoke was coming from one of the chimneys. An ornate sign saying 'Orchard Cottage' hung from the gate, but the fields surrounding the cottage and its gardens were empty and ploughed in frozen grey furrows. There was no sign of an orchard.

'We need to get a bit closer,' said Sienna. 'We can't just wait out here for the next few hours. Let's see if we can get next to the house so we can have a look through one of the windows.'

Sophie could feel the fear rising up inside her. If they encountered Osorio now, she wasn't sure what their next move would be. There was no plan. They hadn't talked this through. She glanced all around her, hoping they could be in and out of there as quickly as possible.

They crept along the hedge that bordered the garden then climbed over a small fence at the side of the house. It was deathly quiet. Sienna lifted her head and peered in through one of the windows. Everything looked just as they would have expected. There was a roaring fire in the sitting room grate that looked very enticing in this grey December weather. The room looked lived in. An elderly lady was asleep in an armchair, and a television flickered in the corner.

'Well,' Sienna whispered. 'Unless that's Osorio's mother, I don't think we're going to have much luck here.'

'We should be getting back then,' said Sophie. 'I think the heavens are about to open and we're going to get soaked.'

Sienna peered in through the window once again, hoping to see something that would make their journey worthwhile, but to no avail.

'Can I help you?' said a croaky voice from somewhere nearby.

When they spun around, an elderly man was standing

at the other side of the fence. He was grim-faced, and he was holding a shotgun.

'Oh hello,' said Sienna. 'We're lost. We were just wondering how to get back to the main road.'

The man glared at her in contempt.

'And did you think you'd be able to find out by peeking in through someone's window?'

The girls didn't respond.

'You kids think you're very funny, don't you?' the man said, 'but some of us don't appreciate your pranks. Putting glue in our locks, plugging up the drainpipes, egg throwing. You've turned my wife into a nervous wreck. She feels like a prisoner in her own home. But you've trespassed on my property for the last time. This time, I'm going to make sure you don't get away with it.'

'Look, I don't know what you're talking about,' said Sophie, feeling a little alarmed. 'We were just trying to find our way back to the town.'

'Well, we'll let the police decide that, shall we?' said the man. 'Until they arrive, I've got just the spot for you two.'

He pointed his shotgun down the side of the house and motioned for the girls to move in that direction.

'Move!' he said, stepping back to keep an eye on the girls.

They walked down the side of the house and out into a yard at the rear. There was a brick-built storehouse about twenty feet from the house and a tractor and some other farming equipment parked nearby. The man unlocked a padlock on the storehouse door and motioned for the girls to step inside. Then he closed the door and replaced the padlock, tugging at it a few times to make sure that it was securely locked.

'You can cool your heels in there for a while,' he shouted. 'Once I've had a bite to eat, I may get around to calling the police.' Then they heard him walking back up the garden path and into the house.

Sophie took her phone out and turned on the flashlight, recoiling in horror at the sight of the spider's webs that clung to every corner. The air smelled stale, musty and damp and so much stuff was crammed into the storehouse there was barely room for them to stand up. Old and broken-down farming equipment rubbed shoulders with a selection of rusty tools. An ancient bicycle was leaning against the wall, and several piles of old farming magazines were stacked in the corner. They all vied for space with the strings of onions that hung from the ceiling and the crates of vegetables that had been stored for the winter.

'We've got to get out of here,' said Sienna, looking uncharacteristically worried.

'But the police will know we weren't the ones who've been vandalising his farm,' Sophie answered. 'They'll let us go without too much trouble.'

'But they'll want to check out who we are first, and my orders are to keep well away from the police while I'm here. There are no records of me anywhere in your world, and that's going to make them a bit suspicious. We have to get out of here before they arrive.'

Sienna's superiors had warned her that she must not get involved with the British police for any reason. The existence of Galacdros and the relationship between the two worlds was something very few people knew about. If her true identity were to be discovered, the security services would deny all knowledge of her.

She leaned all her weight against the door to check how securely it was locked, but it didn't budge an inch. There had to be another way out. Sophie shone the flashlight around. There was only one window. It was quite small, and it didn't open. It was only there to let in the light. Sienna examined it to see how securely it was fitted into the brickwork and concluded that the storehouse was probably something that the farmer had built himself. The screws that held the window in place were still visible above the frame. With the right equipment they might be able to remove them.

They searched through the collection of rusty tools that were scattered around on the floor, looking for anything that might be able to do the job. Ideally, it needed to be a flat-head screwdriver, but anything that could get some purchase on the screws would probably work. It was a fruitless search, though. There was nothing of use amongst the rusty collection. It was all too clunky and thick to get into that little groove.

Sophie felt around in her pocket and pulled out a small bunch of keys. She tried to use the little ring that the keys were attached to but, even though it slotted into the groove quite easily, she still couldn't get the screw to turn.

A flash of lightning briefly cast some light in through the window. Seconds later, they heard the distant rumbling of thunder. Overhead the rain was pattering against the metal roof of the storehouse, and a small leak had allowed a constant drip to develop above Sienna's head. She reached up and wiped the rain off her scalp then carried on with her search for the makeshift screwdriver.

This was all taking far too long for Sienna, and she was becoming a little panicked. She scrabbled at a collection of rusty old gardening equipment, frantically searching for anything that might help. Buried in at the back, she found a small cardboard box that contained hundreds of flat metal discs with a hole in the middle.

'One of these might work,' she said, opening up the box of tiny washers.

When she picked one out and started working on the head of a screw, it began to turn almost immediately. Within a minute she had two of the screws out and was working on a third. Soon that was also out, and there was only one more screw to go. But the last one wasn't so easy. They tried for several minutes, but nothing would budge the final screw that held the frame in place.

Sienna was getting more and more agitated. She was aware that the farmer could return at any minute, and her movements were becoming jerky and frantic. Gritting her teeth, she tried to rock the frame back and forward in an attempt to loosen up the screw, but she couldn't get any movement at all. She kicked the door in frustration.

'There has to be a way to get that screw out,' she shouted, beginning to lose control.

It was a shock for Sophie to see Sienna so off balance. Normally she was so calm and rational and not at all prone to emotional outbursts.

'Don't worry, Sienna,' said Sophie, 'we'll get it out.' She searched around in her pockets, hoping to find something that could move the last screw. 'What about having a go with this ten pence coin? It's a bit bigger than those washers, and we might be able to get a better grip with it.'

Sienna's eyes lit up upon seeing the coin. 'Give it a go,' she said. 'That might just work.'

Sophie pushed the coin into the slot on the head of the screw and tried desperately to get it to turn. It moved fractionally. Sienna had a go and got a little more movement. Her fingers were sore from gripping all the tiny makeshift screwdrivers, but she was determined to get the final screw out.

'Try moving it the wrong way,' said Sophie, 'in case it just needs to be loosened up.'

Sienna put all her effort into tightening the screw. After a few seconds, it shuddered slightly and made a grinding sound. Her eyes widened with hope. She tried turning it back the other way. The screw jolted, then turned a little, and suddenly it was moving freely.

Within seconds she was able to twist it out using her fingers. Her relief was overwhelming.

Shuffling the window frame towards them, they pulled it out of the wall and Sienna poked her head out into the wet and windy backyard. It was late afternoon, and the rain was now coming down quite hard. It battered against her head. Within a few seconds, her hair was completely drenched. She ducked back inside, built a small stack of crates under the window then hauled herself through the gap, landing softly on the saturated ground outside.

'Before you get out,' she whispered back to Sophie, 'hand me out the frame.'

Sophie handed the window frame out to Sienna then climbed through the gap to join her. Once she was on the ground, they slid the frame back into position in the wall.

'He may not notice the missing screws for a while,' said Sienna, 'so he'll have no idea how we managed to escape from his prison. That should give us a head start.'

No sooner had she finished the sentence, when the back door of the house opened, and the farmer appeared, framed in the light from the doorway. He was still carrying his shotgun, and he wore a large weatherproof jacket with the hood up. He started walking towards the storehouse, stopped just outside and rapped on the door.

'I've been having a think,' he shouted. 'I'm sure you two aren't the ringleaders. If you tell me who the rest of your gang of hooligans are, I'll let you two go. What do you think?'

When he didn't get any response, he banged roughly on the door again.

'You should be grateful I'm giving you a choice!' he shouted angrily. 'You and your friends have driven me and my wife mad with your campaign of vandalism. Thanks to you we might have to sell up after thirty years of farming here.'

He waited for a response, but Sophie and Sienna stayed perfectly still.

'I could leave you two in there all night, you know,' he shouted. 'I'm perfectly within my rights. You were trespassing on my land.'

Sienna motioned to Sophie that they should move off towards the hedge that ran along the other side of the garden. At any minute, the farmer might realise that they weren't inside the storehouse, and before that happened, she wanted to use the darkness to get as far away from the farm as they could.

They were both soaking wet, and it was tricky moving around on the uneven, saturated earth, but the noise the rain was making masked any accidental sounds they made. Eventually, they reached the other side of the hedge and started creeping slowly back towards the road. As they did, there was a deafening clap of thunder, and the whole area was briefly lit up by a flash of lightning. Noticing some movement in the corner of his eye, the farmer glanced to the side. For a split second he could see the girls making a hasty exit. He acted instinctively. Without thinking about what he was doing, he turned and fired his shotgun into the darkness.

Sophie dived to the ground, praying that he hadn't hit his target. What an insane thing to do. Fire a random shot at two defenceless strangers. She wanted to leap to her feet and flee into the darkness, but she was so frozen with fear that she couldn't move.

'Think you can outsmart me, do you?' shouted the farmer. 'Well, let's see how you like it when you're the ones who are being chased and terrorised.'

Chapter Four

Sienna dragged Sophie back onto her feet, and they ran across the field towards the massive overgrown hedge that bordered the road. They knew they couldn't use the one-track road to try to make it back to the town. That would be the first place the farmer would go looking for them. There had to be another route back. In the murky light, they could see the outline of a copse of trees a little further down. They ran as fast as they could in its direction.

The rain was now torrential. It battered against the girls ferociously, washing the mud from Sophie's clothes where she had thrown herself onto the ground. Lightning continued to flash and crash overhead, exposing the girls as they ran across the field. Sienna barged Sophie to the ground as another shot rang out. The farmer seemed to have totally lost control. If he hit one of the girls it would be cold blooded murder.

When they finally reached the copse of trees, it provided a little shelter from the battering they were getting from the rain, but they knew they couldn't wait there for long. The farmer had seen them running towards the trees, and before too long he was bound to be on their trail. One more lightning flash at the wrong time, and they would be sitting ducks.

'We've got to do something about him,' said Sienna. 'Every time there's a flash of lightning, he gets a free shot at us. We've got to use the darkness to stop him.'

She looked around for anything they could use as a weapon and found a stout branch that could do some damage.

'This will do,' she said, holding it with both hands and taking a few practice swings.

'Yes,' said Sophie, 'but how are we going to get close enough to use it?'

Before Sienna could answer, they heard the rumbling sound of an engine and the glare of lights as a vehicle moved across the field in their direction. When the area lit up with another flash of lightning, they could see the farmer trundling towards them, sitting on top of his tractor. He looked completely deranged. He stopped halfway across the field and aimed his shotgun at the copse of trees. The girls threw themselves to the ground behind the trunk of an aged oak tree as another blast from the shotgun ripped through the air.

'We're going to have to make a run for it,' said Sienna, 'but make sure you're not running in a straight line. Keep zigzagging so he can't get a proper aim.'

They bolted out of the trees into the darkness, running towards the overgrown hedgerow at the other side of the field. The sound of another shot filled their ears as they zigzagged across the sodden earth. It was a massive relief when they realised the farmer had missed his target once again.

It was heavy underfoot. The rain had soaked the roughly ploughed field, and on the uneven ground they were constantly stumbling in the darkness. In her desperation to move at top speed, Sophie tumbled to the ground, and as she hauled herself to her feet, she turned and looked back at their pursuer. The tractor was gaining on them. Its headlights were on full, and she could hear the farmer laughing as he drove towards them at full tilt.

'We have to split up,' Sienna shouted, 'we're making this too easy for him.'

She darted off at an angle, and the tractor slowed for a moment. The farmer seemed unsure of which girl to go after. Sophie hadn't slowed down at all, though. She was powering towards a gap in the hedge, hoping to find a way to shake the farmer off. No sooner had she made it through the gap when her foot slipped on the sodden earth, and she crashed to the ground and started careering down a steep incline on the flat of her back. It was so dark she couldn't see where she was going. Seconds later, she plunged into a shallow pool of water that had gathered at the bottom of the slope.

At the top of the incline, the tractor stopped by the gap in the hedge. Its lights blazed into the darkness above her. Scrambling out of the water, Sophie ducked behind a cluster of bushes, trying to make herself as small as possible. Her heart was pounding in her chest, and she was finding it hard to catch her breath. Up above, she could see the farmer pacing around at the brow of the slope, shining a flashlight down into the darkness. She crouched down low, shaking with terror as the light danced around in search of her.

'I know you're down there, Missy,' the farmer shouted. 'And I'm not leaving here until I've found you.'

Sophie could see his outline silhouetted against the

lights of the tractor. He was stalking the top of the slope; his shotgun in one hand and flashlight in the other. As the rain battered against his head, she thought he cut a nightmarish figure, like something out of a horror movie.

The flashlight danced across the bushes she was hiding behind once more. Then it paused for a moment and held steady.

'Well, well,' he shouted. 'I think we've found our fox.'

Sophie's heart was beating so fast she thought she might pass out.

'I'm going to count to three, and if you haven't shown yourself by then I'll be putting both barrels of this little shotgun into that bush you're hiding in Missy. One……. Two……'

He never managed to reach three. A thick branch clattered against the back of his head and sent him tumbling down the incline towards Sophie. Seconds later, she could see the silhouette of Sienna at the top of the hill, still holding the branch that had put an abrupt end to the terror of the countdown.

Sienna half-walked half-slid down the slope until she reached the prone body of the farmer. He was lying on his back with his feet pointing towards the top of the hill. His gun was lying several feet away from him, submerged in a deep pool of water. As she knelt over the body, she was joined by Sophie. They were both struck by how much the farmer smelled of alcohol.

'Well, he seems to still be breathing,' said Sophie. 'Do you think we should try to get him to a hospital?'

The farmer stirred and opened his eyes a little. He seemed a bit confused. When he recognised the girls, he tried to sit up, but the searing pain in his head caused him to slump down onto his back again.

'You little punks!' he grunted through gritted teeth.

The girls turned and sprinted back up the hill. When they looked down, they could see the farmer slowly getting to his feet, rubbing the back of his head and looking around for his gun. They didn't wait around to see whether he found it. They darted back through the gap in the fence, past the tractor with its engine still running and headed towards the road. At the last minute, Sophie stopped and grabbed Sienna by the arm.

'Just a minute,' she said, turning and bolting back the way they had come. Seconds later, she returned holding the ignition key from the tractor.

'That should give us a bit of a head start. I think we'll

be much quicker on foot than he will.'

When they finally reached the road, there was a deafening crash of thunder and a flash of lightning that lit up the whole area. As it did, Sophie looked back towards the field. The farmer was now sitting on the seat of his tractor, staring straight ahead of him. He seemed unaware of the torrent of rain that was battering against his head. It was as if it was a warm, sunny day, and he was sitting on his throne surveying his empire. He looked utterly insane.

Chapter Five

As she sat eating breakfast the following morning, the image of the farmer sitting on his tractor in the torrential rain kept flashing back into Sophie's mind. Despite the terrifying events the girls had been through, she couldn't help feeling sympathy for the poor man. After thirty years of farming the same land, he and his wife could be driven from their home by the pranks and bullying of local teenagers. One person's fun was another person's torment. It was no wonder he was beginning to lose his mind.

At the other side of the breakfast table, Sienna was studying the list of addresses Jutan had given them the previous day. There was a fair chance that Osorio was staying at one of these locations, but which one? She furrowed her brow and handed the list to Sophie.

'Do you think we'll be able to take a look at any of

these while we're staying in London?' she asked.

Sophie scanned the list. Her knowledge of London was pretty good, and she quickly managed to work out where most of them were.

'There are one or two that we could check out,' she said, 'but London's a big place and most of them are probably too far out. This apartment block on the South Bank is quite close to the hotel, though. We should be able to walk to that one.'

She paused for a moment and looked thoughtfully across the table.

'Sienna,' she said. 'When you do eventually catch up with Osorio and recover The Orb, will you be going back to live in Galacdros?'

Sienna stared blankly back for a moment. She was so single-mindedly focussed on her mission that she was a little wrong-footed by Sophie's question.

'Erm, I suppose so,' she answered. 'To be honest, I hadn't really thought that far ahead.'

There was an awkward silence for a few seconds. Sophie wasn't sure what to say. In the last five months, they had been through so much together that she couldn't imagine life without Sienna.

'I'd miss you if you weren't around,' she said.

Sienna smiled across the table and reached out a reassuring hand.

'Yeah, me too,' she said. 'But I've no plans to leave at the moment, so let's just enjoy our trip up to London.'

The door to the kitchen swung open, and Mr Watson appeared, dressed in a suit and a brightly coloured tie.

'Come on, you two,' he said. 'If you want a lift to the station you'd better get a move on. I have to leave in a few minutes.'

Sophie's dad had offered to drive the girls to the station before he headed off to Bristol for a business conference. He had already loaded their bags into the back of the car, and he was now waiting impatiently for them to get themselves ready.

'And your mum phoned a minute ago,' he continued. 'She left some important papers behind when she rushed off this morning. She asked if you could take them down to the House of Commons once you've checked into the hotel.'

He handed the girls a fat cardboard folder with the words 'Deforestation Report' typed onto a white label on the front.

'There's an urgent debate taking place in Parliament later this afternoon,' Mr Watson continued, 'and she wants to be sure she has all the facts at her disposal.'

'No problem,' said Sienna. 'We'll run it down to her as soon as we get there.'

She took out her phone and sent a text to Sophie's mum, confirming that they had the folder and would deliver it to Parliament later that day.

'I'm sorry I won't be joining you and your mum at the hotel,' said Mr Watson. 'I'll definitely be back in London by Friday lunchtime though. I wouldn't want to miss out on that trip to Downing Street.'

'That's OK, Dad,' said Sophie. 'I'm sure we'll be able to keep ourselves amused.'

Ever since Sophie had received an invitation to have tea with the Prime Minister, she had been eagerly looking forward to travelling up to London. She was keen to see the inside of such a famous political residence and just as excited to be staying in a luxurious London hotel for a few days.

Sophie's dad would be away on business until Friday morning. As her mum would be working late at the House of Commons for most of the week, it was decided that Mrs Watson and the girls should stay at a London hotel for a few days. The girls could spend some time Christmas shopping and seeing the sights of the capital, and in the evenings the three of them could have dinner together at the hotel.

'So what's it like in London then?' Sienna asked, aware that Sophie was having difficulty containing her excitement.

'It's brilliant,' Sophie answered. 'It's big and exciting, and there's always so much to do. It's the greatest city in the world.'

Sophie loved the intensity and bustle of the nation's capital. The theatres and art galleries, the historic buildings and fantastic array of shops, it was a buzzing, intoxicating city and she enjoyed every minute she spent there.

As they boarded the train at Hampton Spa station, light speckles of snow fluttered down onto the already frozen ground. It had been a cold December so far. With only seven more days to the start of the festive season, it was looking more and more likely that the country might experience a white Christmas.

For the first part of the journey, they were travelling through farming country with field after field of neatly ploughed frozen earth. The land appeared to be in hibernation. Nothing grew, and nothing stirred. From time to time they passed pastureland where groups of sheep nibbled at the frosted stumps of grass, and cows gathered around a snow-flecked hay feeder. They huddled together for warmth, and their movements were slow and deliberate.

Small villages and slightly bigger towns flashed past. Then as the train reached the outer fringes of the city, the landscape started to change quite rapidly. Initially, it was clusters of houses huddled together into small communities, but soon the first of the high-rise apartment blocks appeared, and within minutes they were cutting through the urban sprawl of the suburbs. Concrete as far as the eye could see with lines of cars, trucks and buses slowly snaking along, squeezed between the gaps in the rows of tightly packed houses.

To the north, Sophie could see the towering skyline of Canary Wharf, the gleaming financial centre of London, and soon they were into the heart of the city where the traditional architecture of centuries past rubbed shoulders with the follies and curiosities of London's modern-day creations.

They disembarked at Charing Cross station and walked out onto The Strand, the famous London Street that runs from Trafalgar Square to Waterloo Bridge. Sophie found it thrilling to be in the middle of such a thriving city again. It was vibrant and breathtaking, and even though Sienna found the noise and intensity of it all a little disconcerting at first, she had to admit it was exhilarating to be so near to the seat of power.

'What's that big monument over there?' Sienna asked, pointing at the massive column in the middle of Trafalgar Square.

'That's Nelson's Column,' said Sophie. 'It's a tribute to Lord Nelson. He was one of Britain's greatest naval commanders.'

'What did he do to become so famous?'

'He defeated the French at Trafalgar.'

'But I thought you liked France,' said Sienna.

'I do.'

'So why were Britain and France fighting one another then?'

Sophie thought for a minute.

'Well, you know what boys are like,' she said, smiling back at her friend.

Sienna chuckled. She was none the wiser, but perhaps Galacdros and planet earth weren't that different after all.

After a short walk down The Strand, they arrived at the Imperial Hotel. It was a majestic nineteenth century building that had been renovated in recent years, yet it still managed to retain the regal charm of the Victorian era. The lobby was plush and opulent and large enough to get lost in. Sophie was determined to soak up every luxurious minute.

Their rooms were just as impressive, with views over the street that gave them a birds-eye view of the drama that was playing out down below. Red London buses crawled through the throng of city traffic, while an athletic rickshaw driver swerved in and out of the lines of vehicles, keen to find another fare to ferry around the capital. Sophie couldn't wait to get out onto the street. It was buzzing with activity and she was keen to soak it all up. She spread the map of central London out onto her bed.

'Look at this,' she said. 'Everything we want to see is so close to the hotel.'

'Yeah, well before we do anything,' said Sienna, 'we have to take that folder down to your mum. She needs it to prepare for the debate that's taking place later this afternoon.'

Sophie folded up the map and stuffed it into her backpack, along with her mum's folder and a couple of bottles of water. With spirits high, they left the hotel and stepped out into the babble and hum of the city.

It was a crisp and chilly afternoon. They crossed Trafalgar Square then turned left into Whitehall and headed on down towards Westminster. The area was teeming with tourists. In the happy holiday atmosphere nobody seemed to be in a hurry. Perhaps it was because it was so close to Christmas. Or maybe Sophie was so intoxicated by her surroundings that she only saw the good in people and was glad to be able to take her time and let it all seep in.

Outside Horse Guards, a mounted trooper of the Household Cavalry was doing a sterling job keeping his horse calm, as tourists swarmed around them taking selfies and organising friends into group photos beside the horse. There was a sign on the wall that said 'Beware. Horses may kick or bite.' Nobody seemed to be paying it any attention.

Two elderly tourists were standing by the side of the road, studying a map and looking up and down Whitehall in confusion. Sophie was about to go over to offer them some assistance when a man on a small motorbike pulled over and started chatting away to them good-naturedly. It was light-hearted banter, and he looked as if he was keen to help. But just as the woman leaned forward to hand him the map, he wrenched her bag from her shoulder. And before she could react, he turned away to speed off into the traffic.

In the shock of the moment, nobody moved for a second or two, which should have given him the time to make his getaway. But as he tried to duck in-between the oncoming cars, a London taxi pulled sharply across in front of him. In the seconds that he was delayed, Sienna saw the chance to make her move.

She leapt over a cluster of upright litter bins and clattered into the man, knocking him off the motorbike and sending him sprawling headfirst into the road. He was on his feet again in an instant, still holding onto the bag. As Sienna tried to get to her feet, he aimed a kick at her, narrowly missing her head. Fortunately Sienna had trained for these moments many times, and she was ready for him. She grabbed hold of his foot as it flashed past her head and twisted hard, pulling him off balance and sending him tumbling to the ground once again.

By now, Sophie was also on the scene. She grabbed hold of the strap of the woman's bag and ripped it from his grasp, causing most of the contents to spill out onto the ground. This wasn't how the man had intended things to go. Aware that he was now losing the fight, he leapt to his feet and pulled out a long-bladed knife which he slashed at Sienna, narrowly missing her neck.

'He's got a knife!' shouted one of the tourists. 'Stand back, stand back; he's got a knife!'

Sienna knew they were now playing for very high stakes. One wrong move and it could be her last. She started to circle him, keeping her eyes firmly fixed on what she could see of his face through the gap in his crash helmet. It would be pointless trying to aim a blow to the head. She would have to find another way to overpower him.

The man lunged. Sienna danced back out of range. He lunged again. At the moment that he was slightly off balance Sienna saw her chance. She blocked his thrust with her left arm and struck him hard in the solar plexus with her fist, causing him to gasp with the pain and stagger backwards in shock.

In a state of panic, he leapt onto the prone motorbike and burst forward into the bustling throng of traffic. Cars had to brake and swerve suddenly to avoid a collision, and a cacophony of car horns sounded in anger and frustration. It was all over in a matter of seconds. The attacker had blended into the traffic and disappeared.

Kneeling on the ground by the side of the road, the

tourist whose bag had been snatched started gathering up her belongings with the help of her elderly friend. As she did a policeman arrived on the scene, attracted by the hubbub of activity he had seen from further down the road.

'Are you OK, madam?' he asked, bending down to help the woman back onto her feet.

'Someone tried to rob me,' she said. She was badly shaken and trying hard to hold back the tears. 'And he'd have gotten away with it if it wasn't for these two girls.'

But when she turned around, Sophie and Sienna were nowhere to be found. They had vanished into the hoard of dawdling tourists and melted into the crowd.

Chapter Six

Everything had happened so quickly. One minute the girls were enjoying a peaceful walk through tourist London, and the next they were battling with a knife-wielding thief. Sienna had acted on instinct. She launched herself into the fray without giving it a second thought, but when she saw a policeman approaching, she knew she had to get right away from there. There was nothing to be gained from getting involved with the authorities. The woman still had her bag, and nobody had been hurt. That was all that mattered.

'I'm sorry for dragging you away like that,' she said. 'I couldn't get involved in a discussion with that policeman though. He'd have started taking witness statements and asking for my personal details, and I can't possibly get into all that stuff.'

Keeping her true identity a secret was a constant

problem for Sienna. Even Sophie's parents weren't really sure where she was from. In fact, when she first started working for Mrs Watson she was reluctant to make it an official appointment. She knew she would need special security clearance to be able to visit the House of Commons, which could have thrown up some very awkward questions about her origins. But Jutan made high-level contact with the British Intelligence Service, and Sienna's security clearance was rubber-stamped without investigation. Now Sophie would be able to visit Parliament as a guest of Sienna's, and they could both take the file to her mum's office.

When they reached Westminster, they skirted around the edge of Parliament Square and headed towards the entrance to the House of Commons. Sienna took out the lanyard containing her security pass and hung it around her neck, making sure it was in full view for the security checks. The process still seemed to take forever. Some of the staff were a little nervy and overzealous. They were double checking everything and searching people's bags in minute detail. Sophie wondered whether they had received a tip-off about possible terrorist activity. She was relieved to finally get through it all.

They snaked through the labyrinth of corridors and eventually found Mrs Watson's office which, as she was a new MP, was no bigger than a small storage room. The fact that she had to share it with another new MP made it even more cramped, but at least she had some space to work in while she was in Parliament.

'Thank you so much for dropping this in to me,' said Mrs Watson, gratefully taking the folder from Sophie. 'I should be finished here by about seven o'clock this evening. Perhaps we can all have dinner together at the hotel?'

'Sounds great, Mum,' said Sophie. 'Text me when you're about to leave.'

As they walked back through the corridors of power, Sophie found it thrilling to be able to explore such a famous, iconic building. Decisions had been made inside these two debating chambers that had shaped her country's history and culture. She was awestruck by the immensity of it all and very aware of all the illustrious characters from history who had walked these corridors before her.

They stopped in front of a statue of Winston Churchill, and she tried to explain to Sienna the significance of Churchill to the British people.

'He doesn't look like much of a warrior,' said Sienna, staring up at Churchill's portly frame.

'I think he was more of an inspirational figure than an actual fighter,' said Sophie. 'My granddad used to tell me that Churchill always knew the right thing to say, and he was always there when the country needed a lift.'

As Sienna continued to study the bronze statue, Sophie looked to the side and noticed the Home Secretary Harry Jacobs talking to a middle-aged woman. The woman was eyeing him coldly through narrowed eyes, and Jacobs looked as if he was a little intimidated by her.

Sophie turned her back and tried to listen in on their conversation. Despite the hubbub of noise in the lobby, she was still able to catch a few fragments of what they were saying.

'Well, they won't be able to do much about it if they're without power,' said Jacobs in a low voice, trying to ingratiate himself to the woman.

'Excellent,' she replied.

Sophie thought she sounded Eastern European, possibly Russian, but she couldn't be sure. The woman had a cold and steely manner, and Sophie was surprised that Jacobs was so on edge around her. On television, he always seemed so self assured, to the point of arrogance.

As the lobby became even more crowded, Jacobs ushered the woman into a corner making it impossible for Sophie to hear what they were saying. He muttered furtively to her for the rest of their conversation then he escorted her to the door and she left the building.

'What do you think that was about?' Sophie asked as she watched Jacobs striding back towards the debating chamber.

'That was Harry Jacobs, wasn't it?' said Sienna.

'Yes, it was,' Sophie answered, 'and whatever they were talking about, he was keen to make sure that nobody overheard them.'

'I wonder who the woman was.'

'I don't know,' said Sophie, 'I think she sounded Russian. Why would Harry Jacobs be having meetings with the Russians though? He's not with the Foreign Office. He's the Home Secretary.'

It was all very odd, and Sophie was quite intrigued.

When they emerged back into Parliament Square, the sky had become overcast and grey. It was late afternoon, and as the evening approached the street lights began to glimmer and glow in the gathering winter gloom.

They walked back up Whitehall, continuing to speculate on what Harry Jacobs might be up to. According to Jutan, Jacobs and Osorio were part of a secret society that had a different agenda to the British government. Could Jacobs be working for two sides at the same time? And when he said 'if they're without power' what was he talking about? Whatever Jacobs was planning, Sienna was convinced that he might just lead her to Osorio.

Standing at the lights, waiting to cross the road, she kept trying to piece it all together, ruminating on what the girls should do next. Then a car flashed past them heading south, and it sent her thoughts into a complete turmoil.

If she hadn't heard Sophie's sharp intake of breath, she might have thought she had imagined it, but there was no mistaking the figure in the front seat. The girls looked at one another for a moment; quickly realising they had both seen the same thing. A silver-grey Mercedes had passed through the lights, and in the driving seat was a face they recognised instantly.

'I've just seen one of Osorio's android guards,' said Sophie, wide-eyed in shock.

'Yes, so did I,' said Sienna, 'which means there's a pretty good chance that Osorio is now in London.'

'Maybe he is,' Sophie answered. 'Unfortunately, it looks like the guards are here as well.'

Sienna was undaunted. 'This time it will be different though,' she said. 'By my calculations, there are only two of those androids left.'

Seeing one of Osorio's killing machines again caused Sophie to break out in a cold sweat. The guards were powerful adversaries, built for speed and almost indestructible, and the memory of her last encounter with them was still sharply engraved on her mind.

They were designed by a brilliant scientist called Professor Felso who had been exiled from Galacdros for his experiments with artificial intelligence. He had a unique talent, and Osorio had commissioned him to build a mighty army of androids that would be powerful enough to seize control in Galacdros. In exchange, he offered Felso the chance to return home to continue his experimental work.

Felso soon realised he had made a disastrous mistake. He rebelled against Osorio and helped Sophie and Sienna to escape. In doing so, he signed his own death warrant. The guards were ordered to hunt him down and kill him for his treachery.

Now, the sight of one of these ruthless assassins

driving through central London was a stark reminder to Sophie of their destructive power and their cold obedience to their master.

Later that evening, as they sat in the hotel bistro waiting for Mrs Watson, Sienna was convinced she was on the brink of locating Osorio. She took out the list of addresses Jutan had given them and spread it out on the table.

'So you think this address in Belvedere Road is quite close to here, do you?'

'Yes,' Sophie answered. 'It's on the other side of the river, quite near the London Eye. We could walk over there tomorrow morning and take a look around if you like?'

'I do like,' said Sienna.

Sophie could tell that Sienna was now in hunter mode. Having seen one of the android guards just a few hours earlier, she was convinced that Osorio couldn't be that far away. She was desperate to get started, and the morning couldn't have come soon enough for her.

They were just getting ready to order some drinks when there was another strange turn of events. Sophie looked out through the door of the bistro and, to her surprise, spotted Harry Jacobs. He was sitting in an armchair in a secluded part of the lobby, idly flipping through the pages of a newspaper. She nudged Sienna's arm.

'Don't do anything sudden,' she said. 'I can see Harry Jacobs out in the lobby. He's in a big armchair in an alcove over in the corner.'

Sienna slowly turned her head as if she was aimlessly looking around.

'What do you think he's doing here?' she asked.

A few minutes later, they noticed the Russian woman they had seen at Parliament earlier that day walking across the lobby to join him. She was carrying a briefcase which she put down on the floor in the space between them. The girls watched as inconspicuously as they could, but they were much too far away to be able to hear what Jacobs or the Russian woman were talking about.

After a brief conversation, the woman got up and left, leaving the briefcase behind her. A few seconds later, Jacobs picked up the briefcase and left the hotel. He didn't seem to be his usual swaggering, arrogant self, and he was definitely in a hurry. It was all very strange.

Chapter Seven

It was thrilling to be able to wake up in central London. Sophie felt as if she was right at the heart of everything. She pulled back the curtain and gazed down at the action that was playing out in the street below her. Hoards of office workers were streaming along The Strand, hurrying to get to the warmth of their place of work. Their coats were pulled tight at the collar, and great billowing scarves protected them from the wind. She rifled through her suitcase and picked out her warmest clothes. The girls would need an extra layer today.

When she finally made it down to the bistro, Sienna had already finished her breakfast and looked impatient to get going. Sophie could tell straight away that she was preparing to do battle. There was no small talk from her, just a single-minded focus on the job they had planned for that morning. Sophie had seen her in this mood before. Like it or not, it was going to be an eventful day.

They stepped out into the crisp morning air and headed down towards the river. From time to time, tiny flecks of snow fluttered down from the thick, grey clouds that blotted out the sun and disappeared on reaching the frozen ground. It seemed as if the sky couldn't decide whether to snow or not.

Halfway across Waterloo Bridge, Sophie stopped for a moment and gazed at the magnificent views of London old and new.

'Wow, what a fabulous sight,' she said.

Sienna was looking in a different direction. She was scanning the buildings on the south side of the river, wondering whether any of them would lead her to Osorio.

When they reached the other side of the bridge, they made their way down to the walkway that ran along the south bank of the River Thames. It was already busy. Tourists, undeterred by the icy weather, were happily taking in the sights, soaking up everything the historic city had to offer. They shuffled along in small groups, going nowhere in particular, just enjoying the excitement of being somewhere different for a change.

In the Winter Market outside the Southbank Centre, several of the stallholders were taking a break from setting up for the day's trading. They huddled in front of a food stall, sipping hot cups of tea in an effort to keep warm. The blasts of steam that emerged from their mouths every time they spoke emphasised what a cold morning it was.

It didn't take the girls long to find what they were looking for. Towering over the rolling river was a prestigious development of apartments in a building that looked as if it was once used as an office block. There were views across the Thames to Westminster and Parliament. To the side they could see the massive frame of the London Eye. If Osorio really was holed up in this apartment block, he couldn't have been any closer to the seat of government.

Having circled the building a couple of times, they established that there were only two ways the residents could enter or leave. The front entrance was on the main road that ran from Westminster Bridge to Waterloo. There was also a smaller door at the back that could be entered from the walkway on the South Bank.

'We'll have to split up and take one door each,' said Sienna. 'We can keep in touch by phone and text.'

'Are you sure that's a good idea?' said Sophie, panicked by the thought of being left on her own. 'Wouldn't it be safer if we stuck together?'

'We have to watch both entrances,' said Sienna, 'otherwise we can't be sure whether he's actually here.'

Sophie hadn't anticipated having to do anything by herself. It was daunting enough being on the trail of such a ruthless individual. Now she knew that Sienna wouldn't be beside her, she could feel the fear rising up inside.

'What shall I do if I see Osorio?' she asked. 'Are we going to tackle him out here in the open?'

'No, I don't think so,' Sienna answered. 'For the moment, I just want to establish where he is. Maybe we can follow him and find out what he's up to.'

They agreed that Sienna would watch the front door and Sophie would stay around at the back, an arrangement that Sophie was more than happy with. There were plenty of tourists milling about on the South Bank. She could disappear amongst the crowd and still have a good view of the back entrance.

It was a long wait. Several people came and went at the front of the building, but the rear entrance stayed shut for the entire time. There was a bench a little further down that gave a good view of the back door, but Sophie decided against sitting there. It was too cold to stay in one place for long. She knew it would be much easier to stay warm if she kept moving around. After a while, she took out her phone and thumbed in a text to Sienna.

'No action here,' it read. 'Wish I'd worn a thicker jacket,' followed by a cold-face emoji.

Sienna's reply came almost immediately.

'No sign of him here either. Perhaps he's out buying a scarf and gloves.'

Another hour passed; then another. The girls texted back and forth a few times to keep in touch. There was still no sign of Osorio. Finally, Sienna took out her phone and sent another text to Sophie.

'I think that's enough surveillance for this morning,' it read. 'Why don't you join me at the front?'

It was hard for Sienna to swallow down her disappointment. She had been awake since five o'clock in the morning, imagining herself defeating Osorio and finally recovering The Orb. But three hours in the cold December weather had brought her crashing back to reality. They had drawn a blank, and she was still no closer to completing her mission.

Then, just as she was slipping the phone back into her pocket, a large black car pulled up at the front of the building, and a tall man with a dark goatee beard emerged from the back door. It was Osorio.

'Jackpot,' Sienna whispered, clenching her fist in jubilation. She ducked behind a pillar and watched Osorio as he made his way towards the entrance to the apartments. It had been worth the long wait after all.

Her moment of triumph was short lived. A terrifying figure suddenly appeared to her right and, before she could take evasive action, she felt a searing pain in her upper arm as his gloved hand held her in a vice-like grip. It was one of Osorio's android guards. He pulled her in close and fixed her with an icy stare.

'I have a gun in my pocket, and I will use it if you give me any trouble,' he said, in a monotone, emotionless voice. 'Now, we're going to walk calmly over to the entrance to this apartment block without making any fuss. Mr Osorio is looking forward to seeing you again.'

Sienna knew it would be a mistake to put up a fight. The android was faster and more powerful than her and would have had no qualms about killing her on this busy street in broad daylight. It was just a machine that had been programmed to carry out Osorio's orders. It had no capacity to think through the consequences.

When Sophie turned the corner and saw Sienna in the grip of one of the guards, her thoughts were thrown into a total panic. She thought about rushing over to them, to launch a rescue attempt, but quickly realised that would be futile. The guard would have no difficulty overpowering her as well, and then both their lives would be in mortal danger. She just had to stand back and watch Sienna being marched towards the door of the apartment block.

The guard didn't say a word as he escorted Sienna up to the tenth floor. He didn't even look at her. It was a chilling experience. When they finally reached the apartment, he swiped a security card across the digital lock then dragged her roughly through the open door.

This was not how Sienna wanted to encounter Osorio again. She was totally at his mercy and, at that moment, she couldn't see how she was going to get out of there. As the guard marched her into the apartment and forced her down into a chair, Osorio was standing by the window looking across the river towards Parliament. Determined to exert his authority, he walked over to where she was sitting and towered over her menacingly.

'Search her!' he barked.

The guard went through Sienna's pockets and emptied the contents out onto the table beside her.

'So,' said Osorio. 'We meet again. My associates warned me that someone had been watching this apartment block, and I knew that there was only one person who would be stupid enough to do something so obvious. And it turns out I was right.'

'If I'm so stupid,' Sienna snapped back, 'how was I able to find you so easily? And if I can find you, then others will as well. Until The Orb has been returned to its rightful place in the Senate, we will keep coming after you. We're never going to give up.'

'Ah yes, The Orb,' said Osorio.

He put his hand into the pocket of his jacket and took out a small, smooth stone about the size of a walnut.

'You stupid child! Don't you know that all the time The Orb is in my possession, I can never be defeated? Your attempts so far have been totally ineffective and today will be no different.'

Sienna was enraged at being called a child. She was about to respond to Osorio's jibe when a door at the side of the room opened, and a teenage girl entered. She was small and wiry and about the same age as Sienna. She half smiled, half sneered then plonked herself down sideways into one of the armchairs, dangling her feet over the arm of the chair.

Through the open door, Sienna could see into the other room. There were several laptop computers open on the two desks that were visible, and an empty pizza box was lying on the floor. The girl yawned noisily then let out a belch.

'Who's your friend?' she said.

Osorio stiffened and tried to force a smile.

'This is what passes for a member of The Elite these days,' he said, indicating his head towards Sienna. 'She has interfered with my plans on more than one occasion in the past, and somehow she has always managed to survive. But this time she will not be so lucky.'

'What are you going to do to her?' the girl asked. 'Make her listen to one of those stories about your glorious career? Slow death by boredom?'

Osorio narrowed his eyes then ground out another smile.

'Don't you have work to do?' he said.

The girl stood up and walked over to where Sienna sat. Her small frame was at odds with her belligerent character. She picked up Sienna's phone from the table and scrolled through it for a few seconds.

'Do you play Detonator?' she asked.

Sienna didn't respond.

'No? Pity. I could have saved Mr Grumpy here the trouble and wiped you out virtually.'

Osorio was having trouble controlling his temper.

'Will you get on with your work,' he said through gritted teeth, trying to sound patient. 'You've wasted enough time already on that stupid computer game.'

'Maybe you should spend some time on stupid computer games,' said the girl. 'It might help you deal with your anger management problems.'

Sienna could see Osorio clenching his fists and trying to control his rage. He wasn't used to being spoken to like this, and she wondered why he was tolerating it.

'When Masterson told me you were the famous Nightfly, I thought I'd be working with a computer genius,' he snarled. 'I should have realised you would come with a certain amount of baggage.'

He shook his head and looked at her through narrowed eyes.

'Is there nobody I can work with who will deliver what they have promised? First, I had to put up with that idiot Felso, and now I'm stuck with a girl who has the personality of a four-year-old.'

On hearing the name Nightfly, Sienna remembered the conversation she had with Jutan just a few days ago. This girl must be the hacker who had broken into the computer system at the Galacdros Senate and stolen a lot of sensitive information. And now she appeared to have teamed up with Osorio.

Nightfly slipped Sienna's phone into her back pocket and looked at Osorio with a steely glare.

'So you worked with Professor Felso, did you?' she said, focussing on him intently.

'Yes, I did,' Osorio answered. 'And what a massive error of judgement that turned out to be.'

'Professor Felso was a good man,' said Sienna.

'Felso was a fool,' Osorio spat back at her. 'He picked the wrong side, and it cost him his life. He could have been part of the glorious new order that is coming to Galacdros, but he betrayed me and paid the price for his treachery. But it's no matter. Soon I will possess the plans for the most powerful weapon either of our worlds has ever conceived of, and your father and the other members of the Senate will have to bend to my will.'

Sienna was determined not to respond. She could tell

that all was not well between Osorio and Nightfly. She decided to dig a little deeper to see what she could find out.

'That was you parked by the perimeter fence out by the airport on Saturday, wasn't it?' she said.

'Oh, you witnessed my little audition, did you?' said Nightfly.

'Audition?'

'Yes, his majesty here wanted a demonstration of my computer skills before he was prepared to work with me. So I took that plane out for a little joyride and blew his tiny mind.'

'You could have killed those people,' Sienna snapped.

'What's it to you, Goody Two Shoes?'

'My friend's mother was on that plane, and I don't take kindly to you putting her in danger.'

'Well, you're not really in a position to do anything about it, are you?' said Nightfly. 'So I couldn't care less what you think.'

Osorio had heard enough. Whatever he and Nightfly were planning, he seemed impatient to get started, and he didn't want to waste any more time on Sienna. He checked his watch then turned to the android guard.

'Lock her in the small room at the end of the corridor

and stand guard outside. If she gives you any trouble, kill her.'

As the guard dragged Sienna to her feet, Osorio took a step towards her and fixed her with a venomous stare.

'I am about to show the British government that their security systems are no match for my guile and ambition,' he said. 'Then I will give your father and the other self-interested members of the Senate an ultimatum they would be fools to ignore. But before I do that, I intend to personally dispose of you once and for all.'

Chapter Eight

The guard dragged Sienna down to the end of the hallway then pushed her through a door into a small room. It was barely big enough to fit a single bed and was currently being used as a storage area. There was no furniture in the room, just a series of boxes stacked on top of one another. A mop, a broom and a selection of other cleaning equipment were over in one corner. He shoved Sienna back against the wall, pulled the door shut and locked it.

Down at street level, Sophie had melted into the crowd to give herself time to think. What was she supposed to do now? She had never had to do anything on her own before; Sienna had always been there to lead the way. Now it was all down to her. Glancing nervously around, she checked the faces of the tourists passing by on the South Bank. There could be another android guard out looking for her at this very moment. He could be seconds away, watching her every move. It was a struggle to stay on top of her fear. The urge to turn and run was overwhelming.

She stared up at the monstrous apartment block, wondering how she could possibly break Sienna out of there. It was a daunting task. Even if she did manage to locate her, the idea that she could fight her way in and set Sienna free was laughable. What chance would she have against Osorio's killing machines? And to add to her problems, she had no idea where the guard had taken her.

'Where are you, Sienna?' she whispered. She felt so feeble and helpless.

She was beginning to give up hope when a series of vibrant images flashed into her consciousness. They felt urgent and intense and seemed to be demanding her attention. Could these images be coming from Sienna? Like many people in her world, Sienna was a highly skilled telepath and mind reader, and in the time the girls had known one another she and Sophie had developed a strong telepathic link. Perhaps Sienna could provide the inspiration that Sophie was looking for.

She focussed her attention and tried to allow Sienna's

thoughts to permeate her mind. The images were sharp and detailed. They included a birds-eye view of the river and the London Eye and a small room with an open window. When she closed her eyes, she knew instinctively that Sienna was on the tenth floor, and Sophie could sense that she was in grave danger. Time wasn't on their side. There had to be a way to get into that apartment block.

Almost on cue, a white van pulled up at the rear of the building and two men climbed out. One of them was carrying a small vacuum cleaner, and they both had the words 'Franklin's Domestic Cleaning' written on the back of their overalls. They unlocked the rear door of the apartment block and went inside, leaving the door slightly ajar. Sophie knew this could be the only opportunity she would get. She rushed over to the door and peered inside. There was no sign of the men.

A flight of functional stairs went up to the apartments and down to the basement. Sophie took a few tentative steps inside, hoping it would be obvious what to do next. Within seconds she could hear footsteps on the stairs, and she caught a glimpse of the cleaner heading back down in her direction. There was no time to think about what to do. She darted down the steps towards the basement.

The cleaner went out through the open door. When he appeared a moment later, he was carrying a mop, a bucket and a small ladder. He stopped at the door, pulled it closed behind him and locked it with a key, then made his way back up the stairs. Sophie breathed a massive sigh of relief. So far, so good, she had made it into the building.

Up on the tenth floor, Sienna was pacing around the small room, desperately trying to think of a way out. Whatever Osorio and Nightfly were up to, they could be finished at any minute, and she had no desire to find out what Osorio had planned for her.

'There has to be a way out of here,' she muttered to herself.

The small window that overlooked the river only opened about halfway. There was probably enough room for her to squeeze herself through the gap, but it would be far too risky to try to use this as an escape route. There was very little to grab hold of on the outside frame of the apartment block, and it was a long way to fall to the concrete down below.

Further down the apartment, she could hear Osorio shouting orders in his usual lordly manner and the snap of Nightfly's waspish responses. She wondered why

Nightfly had teamed up with such a ruthless, arrogant man. If she really was the infamous computer hacker Jutan had spoken of, what benefit could there be from teaming up with someone like Osorio?

She was awoken from her thoughts when something clattered against the open window, bringing her back to reality with a start. At first she couldn't work out what had made the noise, but when she pushed her head out of the window it all made perfect sense. A stout rope was hanging down from the roof and it was swaying past the window, banging against the frame from time to time. Could this be the opening she had been looking for?

When she looked up to the top of the building, her spirits were lifted even further. Sophie's head was poking over the edge of the roof, and she was motioning to Sienna to come up to join her. The telepathic message she sent must have got through.

'Oh, Sophie, you're brilliant,' she whispered.

Sienna wasted no time seizing this opportunity. Grabbing some of the boxes that were piled up against the wall, she stacked them under the window to make a step and started edging her head and shoulders out through the small gap.

She must have looked a strange sight to the passengers

on the London Eye and the tourists enjoying a stroll along the South Bank. When they looked up, they could see a girl climbing out of the window of a tenth-floor apartment, and she was holding onto a rope that was hanging down from the roof. Perhaps they thought it was some kind of stunt. Sienna didn't have any choice. She had to go for it. This could be her only chance to escape.

Then, just as she was hauling herself out through the window, the whole of the surrounding area was thrown into complete turmoil. The London Eye stopped turning, the traffic lights on the north side of the river lost their colours, and the fairground rides on the South Bank lost their momentum. It was a full-scale power cut. Now the passengers on the London Eye had a crisis of their own. They were suspended in space, unable to move forwards or backwards. It was as if the entire city was holding its collective breath, transfixed by one girl's daring escape.

Sienna gritted her teeth and tried to focus single-mindedly on the task that lay ahead of her. She was dangling from a rope, more than a hundred feet above the ground. The smallest mistake could be fatal. The icy wind cut through her like a sharp blade. It was hard to get a firm grip on the rope. Within a few seconds, her muscles ached from the strain of holding her own weight. She knew from the challenges she had faced in her training that it was important not to look down. The key to survival was to concentrate on getting to the next level, and then the one after that.

Pushing herself off from the side of the building, she started the nerve-wracking climb. It was a slow process. Using her hands to pull herself up the rope, she walked her feet up the side of the apartment block. The biting cold sapped at her strength. Every step and change of hand position had to be carefully negotiated. There was no margin for error. One slip could be deadly.

Up above her, Sophie was becoming increasingly anxious. It seemed to be taking an agonisingly long time for Sienna to reach the roof, and the pipe the rope was secured around was starting to creak and groan. She crawled over to it, to make absolutely sure it would be able to hold Sienna's weight, but in the split second that she arrived by the pipe it fractured suddenly and came away from the wall.

Sophie reacted instinctively. She grabbed hold of the section of pipe that the rope was attached to and pulled it hard into her chest, clinging on for dear life as she was dragged across the roof towards the edge of the building.

Now she would have to hold the full weight of Sienna to avert a complete disaster.

In a desperate attempt to halt her momentum, she slammed her feet against the parapet at the edge of the roof, straining every muscle and pushing back hard against the wall. She had to hold on. Sienna's life depended upon it.

The suddenness of the pipe fracture had caused Sienna to plunge twenty feet in an instant, and the shock of it almost caused her to lose her grip. As Sophie was dragged across the roof, frantically trying to hold onto her friend's lifeline, Sienna thought she was plummeting to her death. These would be her final few seconds. She would never see Galacdros again, and Osorio would have won. Then just as suddenly her descent was abruptly halted, and it took all of her strength and determination to hang onto the rope.

At the top of the building, Sophie was straining every sinew. She screamed out in panic, imploring Sienna to begin her climb again, knowing that she may not be able to hold on for much longer. But Sienna didn't need to be told. She had already set off and was painstakingly working her way up the side of the building. Every step she took was a step nearer to safety. She could hear

Sophie grunting and straining several feet above her, but she knew that it could be fatal to try to move too quickly.

When she reached the top and grabbed hold of the small wall that ran around the edge of the roof, it didn't come a moment too soon for Sophie. Her strength was fading, and she was struggling to hold onto the pipe. Another few seconds and Sienna may have left it too late.

It was agonising watching Sienna scrabbling at the wall as she tried to haul herself up onto the roof. Sophie wanted to lean forward to grab her arm, but she was frightened to let go of the rope too soon. Even at this late stage, one slip could mean certain death. Finally, Sienna managed to lift her leg over the parapet. She dragged herself up onto the roof and collapsed onto her back in relief.

Sophie was exhausted from her efforts. Her legs were aching from the tension of bracing herself against the wall, and her hands were bloodied from hanging onto the jagged old metal pipe. She slumped back onto the roof and breathed a massive sigh of relief. It was a while before either of them could speak. Eventually, Sophie lifted herself up onto her elbows and examined the bloodied palms of her hands.

'Sorry, I thought that pipe would hold your weight,'

she said, still trying to catch her breath.

'I'm just glad that you could,' said Sienna, smiling across at her. 'You know, you're a lot stronger than you look.'

There wasn't time for them to carry on the conversation.

'We'd better get out of here,' said Sienna. 'As soon as Osorio realises I'm missing those guards will be unleashed again.'

She dragged the rest of the rope back up onto the roof; then they darted down the rear staircase to the door at ground level. Sophie was hoping the door would be easier to open from the inside, but they were out of luck. It was securely locked. Even when Sienna leaned her full weight against it, to see if a bit of pressure from the inside could force the lock, it didn't budge an inch.

'Looks like we'll have to go out through the front,' she said.

There was a plain door a little further down. It opened into a long corridor that led to the front of the building. They crept cautiously forward. At the far end was another door with a small window that overlooked the foyer. Sienna took a quick look through the glass then ducked her head down and leaned back against the wall.

'Well, that's not what I was hoping for,' she said.

'What?' Sophie asked, her eyes widening with alarm.

'One of Osorio's guards is out there, talking to the doorman.'

'Oh no,' said Sophie. 'So what are we going to do now?'

'We'll have to watch them for a while and hope he goes back upstairs. It's not that far to the front of the building. If we see an opening, we may just have to make a bolt for it.'

She checked the security lock on the door. It was just a simple twist-lock to open it from the inside.

'Do you think Osorio knows that you're missing yet?' Sophie asked.

'It's difficult to tell from looking at the guard. They're not really the emotional type, are they?'

Sophie smiled nervously. Despite the difficult predicament they were in, it was a relief to hear a little humour.

She leaned over towards the door and peered out through the window. The doorman was no longer in view. All she could see was the guard standing by the front desk. She was about to look away again when the doorman appeared from an office behind the desk and called the guard over. She watched as they both disappeared into the office, leaving the foyer of the building empty for a moment. There was a split second where she wondered whether they should wait, just to be on the safe side, but she knew this chance might not come again. Grabbing Sienna by the shoulder, she turned the twist-lock on the door and pulled it open.

'Let's go,' she said, stepping out into the light.

Sienna didn't hesitate. The girls rushed across the foyer at full pelt, heading towards the doors that led out into the street. As they passed the front desk, Sophie turned her head to the side, and for a fleeting moment she caught the eye of the android guard. It was a hair-raising experience. There was a slight flicker of recognition on his face that sent a wave of terror surging right through her, but it only served to spur her on even more. She put her head down, kept on running and didn't look back.

Chapter Nine

They sprinted around to the back of the building and blended in with the tourists who were milling about on the South Bank. Several street performers had gathered a large audience around them, and the girls had to dodge in and out of the crowds to make their way along the pathway.

Once they were a safe distance from the apartment, they stopped and leaned against the river wall to take a breather. Sienna turned to look back towards the apartment block. There didn't seem to be anyone following them. Perhaps Osorio hadn't noticed she was missing yet.

'We should be alright now,' she said. 'I don't think they'll manage to find us among all these people.'

Sophie wasn't so sure. She was still feeling panicked, and her heart was pounding away inside her chest.

'That guard in the foyer saw us,' she said. 'In fact, I'm sure he recognised me.'

'He might have recognised you,' Sienna answered, 'but if he wasn't under instructions to stop you, it may not have occurred to him to do anything. They're just machines; they can't think for themselves.'

She took another couple of deep breaths, exhaled loudly and smiled across at her friend.

'Thanks for getting me out of there.'

'I still can't believe I did that,' said Sophie, looking back at the giant apartment block.

'Well if you hadn't I was in big trouble, so I'm very glad that you did. You were brilliant.'

Sophie smiled back at her. 'To be honest,' she said, 'I'm just glad to have both feet safely back on the ground.'

They set off along the South Bank, heading for the Golden Jubilee Bridge. On their way, they passed the stranded passengers who were still stuck on the London Eye. The pods hadn't moved for the last twenty minutes, and a lot of the passengers were now sitting on the floor. It looked as if they were trapped inside giant plastic bubbles, exhibits for the passing tourists to stand and observe.

The Winter Market under Hungerford Bridge was still doing good business, and the tantalising smells of the spicy food and mulled wine reminded Sophie that it had been a long time since she had eaten breakfast. But unusually for Sophie, she didn't feel hungry at all. The adrenaline was still pumping through her veins, and she just wanted to get as far away from danger as possible.

Dodging their way through the market, Sienna filled Sophie in on what had taken place in the apartment, including the meeting with the teenage hacker, Osorio's boasts about a dangerous weapon and the friction between Osorio and Nightfly.

'They're definitely planning something,' she said. 'One of the rooms in the apartment was full of computers, and Osorio said something about finishing their work.'

'We ought to contact Jutan,' said Sophie. 'She'll want to know that we've located Osorio.'

'We can't,' said Sienna. 'Her contact number is on my phone and that's still in the apartment.'

'Couldn't you make a telepathic connection with her?'

'I'll give it a try, but we have no way of knowing whether she has arrived in London yet. If she isn't somewhere close by, then it may not work.'

By the time they reached the north side of the river, the lights had come back on, and the London Eye was slowly turning again. There were still a lot of people waiting to get onto the Eye. It was almost as if they thought the long delay was part of the ride.

'Maybe we should go back to the hotel?' said Sophie. 'We could grab a bite to eat, and you could try to make contact with Jutan.' After the heart-stopping experience they had just been through, she was keen to get right away from there.

But Sienna didn't want to leave while Osorio was still at the apartment. If there was any chance she could get to him and reclaim The Orb, she wanted to stay as close to the area as possible.

'What about that little park?' she said, pointing at a large expanse of greenery a bit further down. 'Let's sit in there for a while.'

They sat on a bench in Whitehall Gardens while Sienna closed her eyes and tried to make contact with Jutan. As she did, Sophie had no option but to sit quietly and listen to her own thoughts. Her mind flashed back to the frantic events she had just experienced on the roof of the apartments. She didn't recognise the girl who had clung onto a pipe while Sienna hauled herself up onto the roof. Six months ago she couldn't even climb a tree. Yet with little thought for her own safety, she had just mounted a daring escape at the top of a massive apartment block. She would never have thought it possible. It was both thrilling and terrifying in equal measure. Slowly she was becoming a different person, or perhaps she was becoming the person she was always destined to be.

They had only been sitting on the bench for about twenty minutes when they saw a familiar figure striding across the lawn to join them. It was Jutan. Sophie was a little taken aback at first. Even though she and Sienna had made telepathic contact a few times during their friendship, she was still amazed by Sienna and Jutan's ability to send their thoughts to one another so easily.

'Hello ladies,' said Jutan, smiling broadly and sitting down beside them. 'To what do I owe this pleasure?'

'We've found Osorio,' said Sienna. 'And I think we've also found out what he's up to.'

'That's excellent news,' Jutan answered. 'And what is he up to?'

'He boasted that he would soon be in possession of the most powerful weapon either of our worlds has ever conceived of, and he intends to use it to seize power on Galacdros.'

On hearing this, Jutan was suddenly grim-faced with concern. Her usual cheery demeanour had completely vanished. 'So it was Osorio who hacked into the secure files at the Ministry of Defence,' she said.

'The Ministry of Defence?' said Sophie, looking a little shocked.

'Yes, I'm afraid so. I've just had a call from one of my contacts at the Ministry, and they're experiencing a bit of a crisis. When the power cut occurred, it took them a few minutes to get their backup generator running, and while their computers were down someone hacked into a top-secret file and copied the design blueprint of a new weapon the British have developed.'

'What is this weapon?' Sienna asked. 'Osorio seems to think it will guarantee him power in Galacdros.'

'It's the most powerful and sophisticated weapon that either of our worlds has ever developed. If Osorio has managed to copy the plans it would be very bad news indeed.'

Sienna stood up and looked through the trees to the other side of the river.

'He's in an apartment over there, on the south side of

the river,' she said. 'And there's a girl working with him who seems to be some kind of computer geek. I think it's that computer hacker you were telling us about. Osorio called her Nightfly.'

'So it's as I feared,' said Jutan. 'They are working together. That's not very good news at all.'

Jutan took out her phone and scrolled through some photos to a close up of two people sitting in a car. One of them was definitely Osorio, and the other was a girl about the same age as Sienna.

'That's her,' said Sienna. 'That's the girl who was at the apartment. And she was responsible for what happened at the airport on Saturday. Apparently, Osorio had demanded a demonstration of her abilities before he would work with her, so she took control of the plane and flew it around for a while.'

'We have to get to that apartment before they manage to disappear,' said Jutan.

She took out her phone and made a quick call, arranging to meet her agents on the south side of the river. Then she and the girls rushed across the bridge to join them.

Sienna found it hard to contain her excitement as they approached the apartment block. There had been opportunities in the past to reclaim The Orb, but this time she had a small team with her. If Osorio was still in the apartment they would have him surrounded. To ensure that Osorio couldn't slip out unnoticed, Jutan posted an agent outside each of the main entrances. The rest travelled up to the tenth floor and prepared to launch their assault.

Outside the door of the apartment, Sophie kept as far back as possible. If Osorio's guards were waiting inside, they were sure to put up a ferocious fight, and she knew only too well what they were capable of. Two of the agents checked their guns and prepared to storm inside, while another took a hefty metal Ram and smashed it into the lock.

When the door burst open the two armed agents rushed into the apartment, training their guns ahead of them, prepared to shoot on sight. But there was no sign of Osorio or Nightfly. They searched everywhere. Sienna was devastated.

In a smaller room off to the side, there were several laptop computers open on two desks. Most of the screens displayed information about the London electricity supply, and on one of them there was an elaborate system of computer coding.

Sophie studied the screens for a few moments. It didn't take her long to work out what it was all about. 'Well, I think this explains why there was a power cut,' she said. 'It looks like it was all controlled from here. They must have hacked into the power supply and shut it down, and in the confusion that followed, they were able to break into the Ministry of Defence computer system.'

She picked up a cup of coffee that was sitting on the table and was surprised to find that it was still quite hot.

'This coffee is still hot,' she said. 'Someone must have been here just a few minutes ago.'

'But how could they have made it out of here?' said Sienna. 'There are agents stationed outside both of the main doors.'

High above them, they heard the sound of a helicopter circling the apartment block. When Sienna looked out of the window, it hovered for a few seconds then it seemed to be coming in to land.

'The roof!' she shouted. 'We've got to get up to the roof!'

Everyone knew immediately what she was talking about. If the helicopter was about to land on the roof, Osorio and Nightfly must be up there waiting for it.

Sienna was determined to get up there before the helicopter could take off again. They bolted up the rear staircase taking two steps at a time and burst through the security door onto the roof. But they were too late. The helicopter had already lifted into the air and was now drifting out into the space above the South Bank. One of the agents drew his gun and prepared to unleash a volley of shots, but Jutan ordered him to hold fire. There were hundreds of people milling around on the walkway down below. They couldn't risk bringing an aircraft down in such a crowded area.

As the helicopter hovered above the crowd, it rotated slightly and Sienna caught sight of one of the passengers. It was Osorio. He smiled triumphantly and gave her a little wave then the helicopter lifted high into the air and headed off towards the east side of London. They had missed him by just a few seconds.

Sophie looked across the river towards the Houses of Parliament and thought about the events the girls had witnessed the previous afternoon. Suddenly the conversation between Harry Jacobs and the Russian woman began to make sense to her.

'Sienna,' she said. 'Do you remember in the House of Commons yesterday, when we overheard Harry

Jacobs say that someone would find it hard to work when they were without power? You don't think he knew there was going to be a power cut do you?'

On hearing the name Harry Jacobs, Jutan's ears pricked up. She listened carefully as Sophie told her of the conversation they had overheard, and of their suspicion that Jacobs was planning something. She was particularly interested in Jacobs' meeting with the Russian woman in the hotel lobby, and the briefcase that appeared to have changed hands.

'We've suspected for some time that Jacobs and Osorio were in contact with one another,' she said, 'so if Osorio was planning to hack into the national grid there's a fair chance Jacobs would have known about it. But your story about the Russian woman and the briefcase is a very worrying development. '

'I wonder what Jacobs is up to,' said Sienna, staring across the river towards Parliament.

'That's what we have to find out,' said Jutan. 'And if Osorio is involved, it's even more urgent.'

'Well in that case, perhaps we'd be better off following Jacobs,' said Sienna. 'We may not know where Osorio is at the moment, but it will be pretty easy to find Jacobs. And if they are in this together, sooner or later they're going to meet up.'

'That sounds like a very sensible plan,' said Jutan. 'But remember, time is not on our side. If Osorio has copied the plans for that weapon, we need to find him with the utmost urgency. And you will need to proceed with caution. Osorio is a ruthless man, and now that he knows you are both in London your lives are in great danger.'

Chapter Ten

Half an hour later, the girls were sitting in a coffee shop in Westminster, eating a late lunch. Sophie made a series of Google searches on her phone and compiled a list of the locations where Jacobs and Osorio were most likely to meet. It wasn't difficult to find Harry Jacobs on any given day. He was the Home Secretary, so it was quite easy to establish where his offices and London residence were located.

'If we're trying to find Osorio as well, it might be better to concentrate on the less obvious addresses first,' said Sienna.

'Well, in that case, perhaps we should take a look at Jacobs' private office. It's in Pimlico, that's not very far from here.'

They walked down Millbank towards Vauxhall Bridge then turned north into Pimlico. It was a quiet residential area filled with tree-lined streets, stately nineteenth-century homes and a smattering of luxury hotels. Directly opposite Jacobs' office, there was a beautiful garden square with enough evergreen trees to convince the girls that it may not be the middle of winter after all. In fact, if it hadn't been for the steady wind, it might have been quite a pleasant afternoon. They sat in the square and kept watch on the front of the building. It soon became clear that Jacobs wasn't the only one with offices in this elegant townhouse. There was an assortment of nameplates attached to the wall next to the door, including a large bronze plaque with H.J. Consulting engraved on it.

Several people came and went as the girls sat and watched the front door. A few of them had to use a wall mounted entry-phone system, but most were able to access the building by entering a code into a push button door lock. By late afternoon, the light was starting to fade. When another visitor approached the door, Sienna squinted and concentrated intently on the woman's movements.

'One, seven, nine, four,' she muttered.

Sophie watched as the woman punched in the numbers. Sienna was right. It was one, seven, nine, four.

Sienna had found a way to gain access to the building. It didn't take a genius to work out what she would want to do next.

'So that's all we have to do to get through that front door,' said Sienna. 'Once we're inside it could be plain sailing from then on.'

'But what if there's someone in there? He may have a secretary. How do we explain what we're doing?'

'We'll think of something,' said Sienna. She stood up and stared at the building through narrowed eyes.

'What if Osorio is in there?' said Sophie. 'What do we do then?'

'Well, there's been no sign of him in all the time we've been sitting here. And I can't imagine Osorio would want to hang around in a small office all day. But there might be something in that office that could tell us where he actually is.'

They left the garden square and crossed over to the large imposing house. Aware that this needed to look as natural as possible, Sienna strode confidently up the steps and keyed the numbers into the lock. One, seven, nine, four. It worked. She pushed the door open and stepped inside.

Sophie wasn't at all comfortable with this. It was one

step away from burglary. They were breaking into private property and, as keen as she was to help Sienna find Osorio, she found it hard to justify what felt like breaking the law. But Sienna seemed determined to press on no matter what the consequences. So with great reluctance, Sophie followed her up the steps and into the hallway.

Compared to the stylish and elegant frontage of the house, the inside was functional and in need of a coat of paint. A series of doors led off the main entrance hall. They were all closed apart from one that seemed to be the waiting room for a chiropractor. There was a large sign on the wall, just inside the front door, displaying a list of the tenants in the property. H.J. Consulting was on the second floor. There didn't seem to be anyone around, so they crossed the hall and quickly made their way up the magnificent wooden staircase.

It was deathly quiet. All the reasons that they shouldn't be there kept crowding into Sophie's mind, drowning out any valiant thoughts or feelings. She could sense the fear rising inside her chest.

It didn't take them long to find Harry Jacobs' office. There was a solid wooden door a few feet from the top of the stairs. It had a beautiful brass door handle and a brass plaque with H.J. Consulting written on it. Sienna tried the door, but it was locked. Before Sophie could stop her, she rapped firmly on the door with her knuckles. To Sophie's relief, there was no response.

'What would you have said if Harry Jacobs had answered the door?' Sophie whispered, still a little shocked. 'Oh hello, I don't suppose you've seen Osorio around anywhere have you?'

'Something like that,' said Sienna, smiling back at her.

They waited for another minute or so. The office appeared to be empty.

'So what do we do now?' Sophie asked.

Sienna took a quick look around, then bent down to look through the keyhole. One of the benefits of being in a Victorian property was that it still contained a lot of the original features, like keyholes and old fashioned locks. She searched through the pockets of her jacket for anything that might help her pick the lock, but without any luck.

'You don't have a hair clip or something like that, do you?' she asked.

'No, I'm afraid not,' Sophie answered, feeling a little relieved. Now that there appeared to be no way into the office, perhaps they could leave before someone discovered they were there.

Sienna stood up and scoured the floor, hoping she would find something that could help her get into the office. Initially the search was fruitless, but further down the hall she discovered two discarded paperclips.

'Oh yes, perfect,' she said.

She shaped the first paperclip into a type of hook. The other she straightened into a continuous wire. Having taken another look up and down the hallway, she put the hooked clip into the lock and dragged it to the side then inserted the straight wire and started jiggling it around.

Sophie was becoming increasingly fretful. She had hoped that they would be in and out of the building in just a few minutes, but this whole process seemed to be taking forever. And now Sienna was intent on breaking into the office.

The tension was ramped up even further when the front door of the building opened and closed and footsteps moved quickly across the tiled hallway. Sophie's heart leapt into her mouth. Someone was coming up the stairs. She took a quick look around, frantically trying to find somewhere for the girls to hide, but there was nowhere in sight.

'Sienna, there's someone coming up the stairs,' she whispered, grabbing hold of Sienna's shoulder.

By the time the footsteps were almost at the top of the stairs, the girls were standing side by side outside the door of H.J. Consulting. Sienna stuffed the paperclips into her back pocket, desperate to hide the evidence.

A middle-aged man came into view. He was a little out of breath from climbing the stairs, but he seemed to be in a cheery mood.

'Good afternoon,' he said, in between gasps for breath.

'Oh, hello,' said Sienna, smiling back at him.

Sophie tried to smile, but she was so frozen with panic she felt as if she had a coat hanger wedged into her mouth.

'Very windy out today,' said the man, still struggling to catch his breath.

'Erm, yes,' said Sophie, a little stiffly. 'But nice to get some sunshine.'

'Yes,' he answered. 'Lovely.'

He smiled as he walked past them, then he carried on down to the end of the corridor where he put a key into a door and let himself in. Once he had disappeared inside, Sienna knelt in front of the lock again and continued to work on the mechanism. Finally, they heard the soft clunk of the lock moving. When Sienna leaned against the door, it swung open.

This was breaking and entering, and Sophie was reluctant to go through with it. She knew that if they were caught, they would be in serious trouble, which wouldn't be good news for either of them and certainly wouldn't be good news for Sophie's mum. The daughter of a new MP being arrested for breaking into the office of the Home Secretary would be all over the papers. Her mum would have to resign.

'I'm not sure we should be doing this, Sienna,' she said, taking a step backwards.

'Well we can't just wait out here in the hall,' said Sienna. 'Either we have to do a quick search of the office or we have to leave. Now that we've come this far, it seems a shame not to take the final step.'

Sophie didn't know what to say. Her loyalties were caught between Sienna and her mum.

'I'll tell you what,' said Sienna. 'Let's give ourselves three minutes to have a quick look around, then we'll go back to the square and carry on with the surveillance.'

Sophie glanced around the deserted corridor. They hadn't seen anyone but the middle-aged man since they first entered the building. Perhaps it would be alright to make a quick search of the office.

'OK, three minutes,' she said. 'And I'll be timing it.'

It was a large room with a high ceiling and magnificent tall windows that overlooked the street. And there was plenty for them to feast their eyes on. The walls were adorned with photos and trophies from Jacobs' glittering career. On the wall above his desk was a photograph of Harry Jacobs smiling and shaking hands with the US President. On the opposite wall, there were several photos of him playing in a polo tournament, including one of him being handed a cup by Prince Charles. He was certainly used to mixing with the high and mighty.

Sienna shuffled through the papers that were piled neatly on the desk. Most of them were to do with his consultancy business, but there was one letter that looked quite different from the rest. It had no letterhead or address of the sender, and it was written in a language that she didn't understand. She handed it to Sophie.

'What language is this?' she asked.

Sophie looked at it for a moment.

'I'm not sure,' she said, 'but I think it could be Russian. It's strange that there's no address at the top of the letter though.'

An envelope from a firm of solicitors was sitting on the other side of the desk. It had already been opened, and the letter that was inside looked as if it had been roughly shoved back into the envelope. Sienna slid the letter out and carefully unfolded it.

'Wow, Sophie, look at this!' she said.

Sophie was a little taken aback by the contents. A central London casino was threatening legal action against Jacobs over unpaid gambling debts.

'How does anyone lose five hundred and seventy-two thousand pounds in a casino?' she said, unable to believe what she was reading.

'Put the letter down and step back from the desk,' said a voice.

The girls gasped and looked across the room to see Harry Jacobs standing by the door. They hadn't heard him come in, and he had caught them red-handed. Sophie immediately thought about her mum and how this would affect her career. She wanted to run, burst out through the door and pretend that this had never happened. But it was too late for that.

'You made a very big mistake opening that letter,' said Jacobs.

He shut the door behind him, pulled a small handgun

out of his pocket and pointed it at the girls. This wasn't the action of someone who intended to bring this matter to the attention of the police. It was far more serious than that. This was the action of someone who had a dark secret and intended to keep that secret well hidden.

Chapter Eleven

'Have you ever heard the expression *curiosity killed the cat*?' said Jacobs. 'If you have, then you really should have learned from it.'

Sienna started to move out from behind the desk, looking for an opportunity to launch an attack, but Jacobs raised the gun and pointed it directly at her head.

'Don't for one moment think that I won't shoot you,' he said. 'The newspapers would have a field day if you were both killed. Two burglars attack the Home Secretary in his private office, and he shoots them both in self-defence. I'm sure I'll look like quite a hero.'

He looked intently at Sophie and a flicker of recognition registered in his eyes. As it did, a smile spread across his reptilian features.

'You're the girl who saved the Prime Minister's life, aren't you?' he said, looking as if he had just won the lottery. Then he turned his gaze back to Sienna. 'And you must be her troublesome friend who I've heard so much about.'

He took out his phone and thumbed in a number, still training the gun on Sienna.

'Of course I could hand you over to the police, but I think I know someone who would be much more interested in seeing you.'

When the call was answered, he turned on the speakerphone. The girls knew immediately who was on the other end. It was Osorio. Even over the phone, he sounded malevolent and evil.

'I've just returned to my office,' said Jacobs, 'and I found that it was being burgled by that girl who saved the life of our glorious Prime Minister. She's with her friend. I'm holding them here until I've decided what to do.'

There was a long pause.

'Would you like me to deal with the situation for you?' Osorio replied eventually.

'That would be very helpful.'

'I'll send someone over to collect them straight away.'

'Excellent,' said Jacobs. 'I'll keep them both here until your people arrive.'

About fifteen minutes later, the girls' worst fears were realised. There was a knock on the office door. When Jacobs opened it, Osorio's android guards entered the room. They showed no emotion on seeing the girls again. This was just another order that needed to be carried out without delay.

They didn't say a word to Jacobs or the girls. They simply grabbed Sophie and Sienna by the arm, marched them down the stairs and out into the street where a white van was parked. There was nobody around, but the girls would have been reluctant to shout out for help even if there had been. The guards wouldn't have thought twice about killing them right there in the street. The presence of witnesses would have made no difference.

From the tall window high above them, Jacobs stood and watched as the guards shoved the girls into the back of the van. Then they started up the engine, pulled out into the traffic and left him to get on with his evening. It was as if they had just collected a consignment of potatoes.

They drove through the streets of London for several minutes. After a bumpy ride, the van finally came to a halt. When the driver pulled open the back door, they appeared to be in a large warehouse. The area was in complete darkness, but a little further down they could see light playing through an open door. It looked like some sort of office. The guards dragged the girls out of the van and marched them through the warehouse towards the light.

Sophie didn't need to be told who was waiting for them. Having heard his voice on the phone in Jacobs' office, she had been dreading coming face to face with Osorio again. He had already tried to kill her twice, but somehow she had always managed to survive. Would this be third time unlucky?

When they entered the office, Osorio was sitting in a large armchair at the far side of the room. He looked like a medieval king sitting at the head of his court, waiting for his troops to arrive with their captives. The guards dragged Sophie and Sienna into the middle of the room then forced them down into two office chairs. As they did, Osorio rose from his armchair and looked on imperiously.

'I'm so glad you've been able to join us here to witness another of my triumphs,' he said.

He turned to Nightfly who was seated at a desk over to one side, engrossed in an open laptop computer.

'Are the plans for the weapon now securely stored?' he barked.

'Relax, Mr Grumpy. They're all here,' said Nightfly. 'No doubt you'll be claiming the credit for this in some future story about your glorious career.'

Osorio gritted his teeth and glared at her. Then he turned to Sophie and Sienna.

'And so to you two,' he said. 'You have been a constant thorn in my side and, to be honest, I'm almost starting to admire your persistence. But unfortunately for you, your struggle is about to come to an end. Tonight, as the city sleeps, you will be going for a swim in the most treacherous part of the mighty River Thames. And if the freezing cold water doesn't put an end to you, then the dangerous undertows and currents undoubtedly will. I suspect it will be several days before your bodies are found, if they are ever discovered at all.'

Sophie bit her lip and tried not to show any fear, even though her insides were churning up with terror. Their situation looked hopeless. They would never be able to overpower or outrun the guards, and she had to fight hard not to surrender to despair. But when she glanced across at Sienna, she wasn't surprised to see her friend staring defiantly back at Osorio, almost daring him to follow through on his threat. Sienna was an unstoppable force with total self-belief, and Sophie knew that she would never give up the fight.

'I'm not usually into gambling,' said Nightfly, looking up from the table, 'but my bet is these two will outwit you just like they did last time.'

Osorio turned towards her and pulled a gun from inside his jacket.

'Well, you'll be in the perfect position to find out,' he said, 'as I think it's only right that you should join them.'

Nightfly was unmoved by Osorio's threat. She smirked and leaned back in her seat.

'Yes, my dear,' Osorio continued, 'now that our work together has been completed I won't have to put up with your abuse and disrespect any longer.' He pointed the gun at her and moved a little closer. 'So, hand over that computer.'

Nightfly stayed where she was and shook her head dismissively.

'I said, give me the laptop,' Osorio barked, becoming increasingly angry. He turned to the android guards with a look of frustration on his face. 'Take the computer away from her and drag her over there with the others.'

But on hearing his orders, the guards started to

behave quite oddly. They turned to one another, bowed their heads and started waltzing around the room to imaginary music. When Nightfly saw the look of confusion on Osorio's face, she leaned forward in her chair and burst out laughing.

'What is this?' Osorio shouted. 'I ordered you to take the laptop from the girl.' He rushed over to the guards and pulled them apart. 'Do as you are told,' he shouted. But it made no difference. The guards just looked at him and smiled.

'Take the gun away from him,' said Nightfly.

Before Osorio could respond, one of the guards had grabbed hold of his arm and taken the gun from him.

'Now tie him to that chair.'

The guards were so powerful that Osorio was in no position to resist.

'What are you doing?' he shouted as they dragged him across to the chair. 'I am your master. I order you to release me and take the computer from the girl.'

It had no effect on the guards at all. Within a couple of minutes, Osorio was securely tied to one of the office chairs and Nightfly was standing over him holding the gun.

'As you can see,' she said, 'I've made a few

amendments to their circuits. They now believe that I am your commanding officer, and they should protect and obey me at all costs.'

Osorio struggled frantically against the ropes, but he was so tightly bound that he was totally immobilised.

'You'll pay for this treachery,' he shouted.

Nightfly shook her head and stared at him with contempt.

'Now, you're probably wondering how I managed to make those amendments,' she continued. 'Well, it wasn't easy. The circuits in their heads are difficult to access, and Professor Felso never revealed his coding secrets to his colleagues back on Galacdros. In fact, the only person he ever shared his knowledge with was his seven-year-old daughter when she sat with him as he worked in his laboratory. He couldn't have known it at the time, but those hours they spent together were some of the happiest times of her life, and they inspired her to become something of a computer wizard herself. She's probably the only person who could have reprogrammed these androids.'

Osorio stopped struggling for a moment as he finally understood what was happening.

'So you're Felso's daughter, are you? Well, that explains a lot.'

'Yes,' said Nightfly, 'I learned a great deal as I watched my father working. And once I found out that you were responsible for his death, I was determined to ensure you never got your hands on the plans for that weapon.'

'Your father was a fool,' said Osorio, struggling against the ropes. 'He could have had a glorious future. He could have shared in our new world order, but he was careless and disloyal.'

'No, that's not true,' said Sophie. 'Professor Felso realised he had chosen the wrong side and did what he could to make up for it. The only reason he sided with you in the first place was so he could go back to Galacdros to see his family again.' She turned towards Nightfly. 'He missed you terribly, and he wanted to apologise for tearing your family apart.'

Nightfly sneered and swallowed hard, pushing her feelings down as far as she could.

'Well, I may never be able to see my father again,' she said, 'but I can still avenge his death.'

She walked over to her backpack and took out a small laptop computer and a thick belt with a series of black capsules attached to it.

'This belt contains enough explosives to destroy this

office and most of the rest of the building. Once I set the timer, it will detonate in thirty minutes.'

She tied the belt around Osorio's torso, making sure it was securely attached. Despite the ropes that were cutting into his arms, Osorio twisted and struggled in a frantic attempt to free himself. He shouted aggressively at the guards, ordering them to set him free. In his desperation, he was becoming a little hysterical.

Nightfly opened the laptop and set it down on the desk. The timer was displayed on the screen. It read 30.00. Then she stood over Osorio and looked coldly into his eyes.

'There is a programme on here that will shortly obliterate your new world order,' she said. 'So it looks like you are going to be playing Detonator with me after all.'

Then she turned to the android guards.

'I will be leaving here shortly,' she said. 'As soon as I have left the warehouse, drive back to the river, jump off one of the bridges into the deepest water you can find and await further orders. These two girls can make their own way home.'

She returned to the laptop and started the countdown. Once she was sure it was operating correctly, she walked over to where Sophie and Sienna were still seated.

'You are free to go,' she said, 'and if I were you I'd get right away from this place as soon as possible. Osorio has arranged to meet Harry Jacobs here shortly, and he's bound to come with his meathead of a driver. Hopefully, they'll be here with Osorio when this bomb goes off because it's going to flatten everything in its path.'

'But we can't just leave him here like this,' said Sophie. 'This is murder.'

'I have my own version of justice,' said Nightfly. 'He was about to murder you and let your body be washed down the river. Why should you worry about him?'

'Because there's a right way to do things, and this isn't it,' said Sophie.

Nightfly didn't respond. She stuffed the gun into her backpack, picked up the laptop containing the stolen plans and turned back to face Osorio.

'You won't need these plans where you're going,' she said, stuffing the computer into her backpack. 'I'd like to say it's been fun working with you, but that would be a lie.'

Then she slipped the backpack onto her shoulder, strode briskly towards the exit and disappeared into the night.

Chapter Twelve

Once Nightfly had left the warehouse, Osorio began to bark orders at the guards in the mistaken belief that they would now obey him. But it was as if they couldn't hear what he was saying. Having received fresh orders, they were determined to execute them without delay. They ignored Osorio and the girls, returned to the van and drove off towards the river.

The digital clock on the laptop was already down to 26.23.

Sienna knew she had to seize her opportunity while Osorio was tied securely to the chair. She frantically searched through his pockets, knowing this could be her best chance to recover The Orb, but she couldn't find it anywhere.

'Where is it?' she shouted. 'Where is The Orb?'

'You'll never be able to find it until you get this belt

off me,' Osorio snapped back at her.

'Tell us where The Orb is and we'll help you,' said Sienna.

'Not until the belt is off.'

Osorio had concealed The Orb inside his jacket, and he was determined to use this as a bargaining chip. If the bomb went off while it was still strapped to him, The Orb would be obliterated and Sienna would have to go back to Galacdros with her mission unfulfilled. She would either have to help him escape from the bomb belt or run the risk of losing The Orb forever.

Sophie looked across at the timer displayed on the screen. Her thoughts were in complete turmoil. In less than twenty-five minutes, the bomb would detonate and destroy the warehouse, killing Osorio in the process. For the first time in five months, she would be free of the constant feeling of dread and her life could return to normal. But however she looked at it, this was murder. Was she really going to stand by and let someone take another person's life? Much as it pained her to help Osorio, she had to do what she could to stop the countdown.

She pulled a chair over to the desk and started examining the laptop. Time wasn't on their side. She would have to move quickly.

'Do you think you can stop the bomb from detonating?' Sienna asked.

'I don't know,' Sophie answered. 'I can poke around and try to find out how she's set up the timer, but there's always a chance that by doing that, I might set the bomb off myself.'

For several seconds she sat in front of the laptop, too frozen with fear to do anything. Despite her prodigious computer skills, Sophie had never had to tackle anything as complicated or dangerous as this before. There were two things she had to find out: where Nightfly had hidden the programme that would detonate the bomb, and how she had synchronised the timer.

Every click of the mouse was a massive risk. She held her breath and inched her way forward, knowing that every move she made could be her last. The countdown was now down to 22.14.

Osorio was consumed by frustration as Sophie slowly and tentatively explored the laptop. He wriggled and struggled against the ropes that bound him to the chair, grunting and snorting as he twisted back and forth.

'If you're going to do something about this bomb, then don't just sit there looking at that computer!' he shouted. 'Get a move on; there are less than twenty minutes left!'

Sophie stared at the screen, desperately looking for inspiration, but wherever she looked, she couldn't find the programme that would detonate the bomb. She furrowed her brow, wondering whether she would be able to do this in time. Perhaps she had overestimated her computer skills and this was way beyond her ability. Every failed search knocked her confidence a little more. But she knew she had to keep searching. She could be only one click away from a breakthrough.

The clock ticked down to 14.27, and she was still no closer to finding the answer.

Sienna was becoming more and more agitated. As the time ticked by, she paced up and down the office, stopping occasionally to look over Sophie's shoulder.

'Couldn't you just turn the laptop off?' she asked.

Sophie looked at her and shook her head.

'It's a sophisticated bomb. It doesn't have an on/off switch.'

A massive list of programmes was displayed on the screen, most of which Sophie had never come across before. She worked her way through them one at a time, Googling the name of the programme to get more information and eliminating them one by one

The countdown was now reading 07:36, and she

wasn't even halfway through her search. Her stomach felt knotted and tense, and it took an enormous effort to stay on top of her anxiety. Back to Google, type in the next name. Find out what it is. Eliminate it from the list of possibilities. Move on to the next programme. The clock kept ticking. 05:37 left.

Osorio was still wriggling and squirming in his chair in a desperate attempt to loosen the ropes that bound him. All of his usual composure had vanished and he was starting to become a little frantic.

Back to Google, type in the next name. F37E442L097S124O12. It seemed like a strange name for a programme. The Google search didn't recognise it, so where did this name come from? And then Sophie had a sudden moment of clarity. She stared at the name again. Take the numbers out of it, and that only leaves five letters. F E L S O.

'Felso,' she muttered to herself. 'Sienna, I think I've found the programme that's running the bomb.'

'Shut it down then!' Osorio shouted. 'What are you waiting for? Just shut it down!'

'I can't delete the programme without deactivating the timer, you idiot!' Sophie snapped back at him. 'It could set the whole thing off.'

The clock was now down to 03:24.

She scanned the rest of the programmes wondering which one was linked to the timer. It would take too long to go through them all. She would have to make an educated guess and hope she got lucky. Nothing stood out. It was beginning to look like an impossible task.

Sienna had seen enough. Much as she wanted to retrieve The Orb, she didn't want Sophie to die for it.

'Sophie, we've got to get out of here,' she said. 'There isn't enough time left to find it now.'

Sophie didn't reply. She was still determined to defuse the bomb. Whatever crimes Osorio had committed, she couldn't just stand by and let him be murdered. She had to continue to try, no matter what he had done to her in the past.

She decided to try something completely different. This would be the last throw of the dice. The countdown was now at 01:18.

She went back to Control Panel and double-clicked Services. As she scrolled down the list, nothing was jumping out at her.

Osorio had now become quite hysterical. 'I demand that you get these ropes off me,' he shouted, rocking back and forth on his chair. 'You can't leave me here like this.'

The clock was now reading 00.27.

It was all beginning to look quite hopeless. Then right at the bottom of the list, two words stood out to Sophie like a red flag. *Windows Time.* She instinctively clicked on it.

'Windows Time is running,' she shouted. 'But why? This laptop isn't linked to any other computers. In that case, there's only one thing it can be linked to.'

The clock was now at 00.09. Sophie knew she would have to take a massive risk. The cursor paused over the list of commands. This could be the last thing she ever did. She clicked 'pause' and held her breath.

There wasn't a massive explosion. When they looked at the clock, it read 00:02. A few seconds later, it still read 00:02.

There was complete silence for a moment.

'Sophie, I think you've done it,' Sienna shouted, rushing over to her friend.

'No I haven't,' Sophie answered. 'I still have to deactivate the bomb.'

One more nerve-tingling moment to go. She went back into Control Panel, found the rogue programme, clicked the mouse, and a list of commands appeared. The cursor hovered for a second over the Uninstall command. She took a deep breath and clicked it. There was no explosion. They were still alive.

Nobody said a word for a few moments. Sophie was so nervous that she was frightened to breathe in case it was still too early to celebrate. Still nothing happened. Finally, she exhaled loudly and put her head in her hands. Her relief was overwhelming.

'You did it,' said Sienna. 'Sophie, you're a genius. You did it.'

But Sophie just sat there, staring straight ahead. Now that the bomb had been safely defused, the enormity of what she had done hit her like a cold blast of air. She started to shake, and it took an enormous effort to fight back the tears. This should have been a moment of celebration. She should have been dancing around the room high-fiving everyone, but it was as if someone had clicked her pause button to give her brain a chance to take everything in.

One massive hurdle had been overcome, but Sienna knew that they still had to deal with Osorio. Somehow they needed to take The Orb from him and make it out of the warehouse before Harry Jacobs and his driver arrived. That was going to be easier said than done.

With the threat of total annihilation no longer hanging

over him, Osorio had now regained his composure. He had stopped struggling against the ropes, and his usual arrogance had returned. He knew the main battle was yet to come.

'So what do we do now?' he said, looking to seize the initiative. 'If you want a chance to take The Orb from me I'm afraid you're going to have to untie me.'

'And if we do untie you, do we have your word that you will hand over The Orb?' Sienna asked.

'No,' Osorio answered. 'But it's the only option you have. If you really want The Orb, you'll have to run the risk of untying me and then try to take it from me. What have you got to lose? There are two of you, after all.'

Before Sienna could respond, they heard a vehicle pulling up outside, and the glare of headlights appeared at the far end of the warehouse. Two car doors slammed. They could hear the sound of voices. And one of them sounded a lot like Harry Jacobs.

Chapter Thirteen

'We've got to get out of here,' said Sophie. 'If that's Harry Jacobs, he's sure to be armed.'

Sienna was heartbroken to have to leave without The Orb, but she knew that Sophie was right. It would be madness to stay on and try to fight it out.

They couldn't go out through the warehouse, Jacobs and his driver had already entered at the far end, so they rushed over to a small door at the side of the office. When Sienna discovered that it was locked, she slammed the sole of her boot into the lock with such savage ferocity that the door sprung open and crashed against the outside wall. With Osorio's shouts ringing in their ears, they burst through the open door and fled into the darkness.

It looked as if they were inside a large trading estate that was surrounded by a high wall. Despite the lack of lighting, they could make out several commercial vehicles dotted around the yard and a row of industrial waste bins over in the corner. In the dim light, it was difficult to move around. The cloud cover had blotted out the moon. With no street lighting able to penetrate the outer wall, it was a while before the girls became accustomed to the darkness.

A commotion of noise was coming from the office as Jacobs and his driver worked to set Osorio free. Before too long, all three of them burst out into the yard. Fortunately for the girls, it took their pursuers a while to get used to the light and for several seconds they were shuffling around in the dark. Then a light appeared from the flashlight on the driver's phone. It scanned the surrounding area, licking into the nooks and corners in an effort to find the girls.

'Spread out,' Osorio shouted, 'they've got to be out here somewhere.'

Sophie could see the outline of his skeletal frame silhouetted against the light shining from the office. Somehow he had managed to remove the bomb belt, and he was now stalking around in the darkness like a giant lizard.

Crouching down behind the industrial waste bins,

the girls knew they didn't have much time to find a way out. It was a cold evening and light rain was beginning to fall. Sophie was sure it was only a matter of time before the flashlight flickered onto the spot where they were hiding. She made herself as small as she could and tried to keep perfectly still.

Despite the gloomy light, they could just make out the craggy features of Harry Jacobs and his driver as they crept around in the darkness. Sophie could see immediately why Nightfly had called the driver a meathead. With his large shaved head and stubby neck, he cut a nightmarish figure as he crept around in the gloom.

As the flashlight danced around, getting ever closer to their hiding place, the girls held their breath, hoping desperately that their luck would endure. Osorio passed just a few feet away from them then continued down the yard, squinting into the darkness. When the silhouette of his frame was caught in the light, they could tell that he was once more carrying a gun.

'You're going to have to show yourselves eventually,' he shouted. 'This yard is totally enclosed by a high wall. The only way out is through the warehouse.'

Sienna knew the girls would have to take a chance at some point. They couldn't just stay where they were. It would be a massive risk to make a run for the warehouse; the light emanating from the door to the office would rob them of their invisibility. There had to be another way out.

She noticed a ladder lying on the ground beside an adjoining warehouse. If they could make it up onto the roof, they might be able to cross over to the other side and drop down into the street. It was worth taking a chance. They had to do something.

Once Osorio was a fair way down the yard, she leaned over towards Sophie.

'There's a ladder over there,' she whispered. 'We could use it to get up onto the roof.'

Sophie swallowed hard and tried not to let the fear overtake her.

'If we could get over to the other side,' Sienna continued, 'we might be able to make it to the road before they realise we're gone.'

Sophie didn't say anything. She just nodded. Despite the horror she felt at Sienna's suggestion, there didn't seem to be any other option.

Over the pitter-patter of the drizzling rain, they could hear Osorio's voice barking out threats from further down the yard. They both knew that this was the moment to make their move. They may never get another chance. Lifting the ladder up as silently as she could, Sienna leaned it against the wall, and the girls climbed slowly up towards the roof. If there had been any decent lighting nearby, they would have been horribly exposed. But in the near darkness, they were able to reach the top without giving their position away.

Sophie couldn't tell whether she was shaking from the cold or from the panic that was now starting to consume her. She had always had a fear of heights. Now she would have to scale a roof in the drizzling rain with three armed gunmen on her trail. She bit her lip and tried to stamp on her emotions. It was hard not to surrender to despair.

To make matters worse, it was difficult climbing up the cold grey slates. The roof sloped at quite a steep gradient and, with very little to hang onto, she was beginning to think that they had made a massive mistake. But she pressed on regardless. Sienna was convinced that if they could just get over to the other side of the ridge, they would be almost free of their pursuers.

If it hadn't been for the light drizzle, they might have been able to make their escape without any problems. But just as they were reaching the ridge at the top,

Sophie's foot slipped on the wet surface. Before she could stop herself, she crashed forward onto the slates and started to slide back down towards the yard.

She scrabbled and grabbed at anything she could get hold of. Nothing could stop her descent. When everything seemed hopeless, she just managed to jam her foot into the surrounding guttering. It stopped her from tumbling over the edge. But in the heat of the moment, she let out a cry of desperation and Osorio was alerted to the girls' whereabouts.

In the seconds that followed, everything seemed to happen in a flash. Sienna slid back down to where Sophie was clinging on and pulled her back into a safe position. They could hear Osorio and the others running in their direction. Their situation was now desperate.

'We've got to get this ladder up onto the roof,' said Sienna, reaching down to grab hold of the top step.

With her heart pounding in her chest, Sophie grabbed hold of one side of the ladder, and they hauled it up towards them. By the time they had dragged it out of reach, Osorio was already underneath. He fired a shot into the space above him, unable to make out any clear shapes, hoping to get a lucky hit. Fortunately for the girls, it disappeared into the darkness.

'They're up on the roof,' he shouted. 'Shine the light up there. Get a ladder.'

The girls scrambled back up the slates, moving more cautiously now and holding onto one another on the increasingly slippery surface. They could hear the driver trying to break into the building down below and Osorio shouting angrily for him to hurry up. Soon they were aware that Osorio was underneath them. Random shots were being fired into the air. One of them blew a hole in the roof just a few inches from where Sophie was sitting, sending shards of slate splintering into her clothes and hair.

Straddling the ridge at the top of the roof, Sienna knew they would now have to scale down the other side, and quickly. It would be a risky thing to do with Osorio down below, listening for their footsteps. Anything that made the slightest noise would alert him to their whereabouts, and they would be sitting ducks. Noticing some fragments of slate and small stones that were caught up in the gaps under the slates, Sienna picked up a handful and put them in her pocket.

It was a slow and painstaking process moving down on the other side of the roof. Frantic activity was taking place back in the yard. They could hear a metal ladder slamming against the wall and Harry Jacobs' voice shouting out instructions.

There was no time to delay. They had to keep moving. Sienna grabbed some of the small stones from her pocket and threw them down to the other end of the roof. Seconds later, the slates were punctured by bullet holes in the exact spot where the stones had landed. The girls kept going, creeping slowly down towards the edge of the roof. When they reached the guttering, Sienna threw some more stones. Again, several bullets smashed through the slates followed by angry shouts from Osorio.

A little further down, a lone streetlamp cast just enough light for them to see that it was still about fifteen feet to the ground. Sophie looked utterly devastated. This was the last thing she had been expecting.

'What do we do now?' she said. 'It's much too far to jump.'

'I'm afraid we don't have any choice,' said Sienna. 'We're going to have to risk it.'

Even though she was as daunted as Sophie by how far it was to the ground, she was determined not to show it. This was a time to show leadership. Sophie was relying on her. Without saying a word, she climbed off the edge of the roof and soon she was dangling by her fingertips with her feet still way above the ground. It was going to be a long drop. Sophie watched in horror as seconds later Sienna let go. She landed with a thud and rolled over on the concrete, but she was on her feet again in a second.

Now it was Sophie's turn. She looked down towards the ground and felt frozen with fear. Sienna had made it look so easy. But Sienna made everything look easy, and this was way beyond anything Sophie had ever attempted in the past. It felt like she was jumping off the top of a house. When she looked behind her, the driver's head was starting to poke above the ridge from the other side of the roof. He would be here any second, and she could see that he was carrying a gun. Either way, she was staring death in the face. She would have to take a leap into the unknown.

For perhaps the first time in her life, Sophie turned off her rational mind and just surrendered to the action. There was no other option. Soon she was dangling by her fingertips. Then she let go. When she crashed to the ground, her ankle turned, and she let out a scream of pain. There was no time to worry about her injury. They had to get out of there.

They picked one direction and ran through the

darkness. They had no idea where they were going. Their only plan was to get right away from there as quickly as possible. The pain in Sophie's ankle ought to have slowed her down, but it was surprising how fast she could run when driven forward by fear.

By the time they reached the main road, they could see the lights of Tower Bridge standing proud above the level of the houses. Sophie darted out into the road and flagged down a passing London taxi.

'Where to?' the driver asked.

'Trafalgar Square, please,' Sophie answered. But she was so relieved to be safely inside the taxi she would gladly have gone anywhere, just as long as it took them right away from Osorio.

Chapter Fourteen

It was a slow start to the day the following morning. As Sophie became accustomed to being awake, images flashed into her mind of the clock on the laptop and her frantic attempts to stop it from reaching zero. She felt as if she was watching someone else. The Sophie she had known for the last twelve years would never have taken such a massive risk.

When she arrived in the bistro for breakfast, Sienna was sitting at one of the tables sipping a cup of coffee. It was already nine-thirty, so most of the business guests had already left the hotel, and the girls more or less had the bistro to themselves.

'How's your ankle?' Sienna asked as Sophie sat down wearily at the table.

'Not as bad as I thought it would be. When we got back to the hotel yesterday, I thought it was going to swell up overnight. But so far it seems to be OK.'

They helped themselves to breakfast from the large buffet that was on display. Having spent a lot of energy over the last few days, they both had quite an appetite. Sophie was struck by how positive and upbeat Sienna was, despite the disappointment she had experienced the previous evening. While Osorio was tied to the chair, she had him at a disadvantage. But she still hadn't been able to take The Orb from him. Yet this morning, she was already planning how they could track him down again. Sophie found it uplifting to be around someone who was always so optimistic and resilient.

'You were brilliant last night,' said Sienna, once they had both finished re-fuelling. 'I thought that bomb was going to wipe us both out.'

'So did I,' said Sophie. 'Let's hope we're in for a more peaceful day today.'

'What do you think Harry Jacobs is up to?'

'I don't know, but whatever it is, he wasn't pleased we found that letter about his gambling debts.'

'He certainly wasn't. And why had he arranged to meet Osorio at the warehouse last night?'

Sophie was about to respond when she felt her phone vibrating inside her pocket. She expected it to be a text from her mum. When she looked at the screen she had a bit of a shock.

'What is it?' Sienna asked. 'Who's it from?'

Sophie turned the screen to face Sienna.

'It's from you,' she said.

'That must be from Nightfly. She took my phone when we first met in the apartment on the South Bank. What does it say?'

Sophie tapped the screen to reveal the message.

'It's just a random series of numbers and letters.'

She put the phone down on the table between them. On the screen was an eleven character code. SE168ZN1130.

'It looks like another one of her number and letter puzzles,' said Sienna.

But the system Sophie used to defuse the bomb the previous evening didn't work this time. When they took all the numbers out, it read S E Z N. They looked at one another, wondering what on earth it could mean.

'Perhaps it's in a different code,' said Sophie. 'Maybe it's like those spy codes where they use numbers to replace some of the letters to make the message look like nonsense. So the first letter of the alphabet is A, the sixth is F, and the eighth is H, and so on. So this would read S. E. A. F. H. Z. N. A. A. C. O. What does that mean?'

'I think it means that's not the code,' said Sienna, smiling back at her.

They stared at it for a while longer. Then another text arrived, and again it was from Sienna's phone. It was another short message but this one was easier to understand. 'Come alone,' it said.

'Come alone?' said Sienna. 'Come alone, where?'

She picked up Sophie's phone and sent a reply. 'Come alone where?' the text read. But there was no response.

Another few minutes passed as they tossed out more suggestions on what the code might mean. Then Sophie had a sudden moment of inspiration.

'Hang on a minute. SE16 8ZN? Perhaps that's a postcode. She might have given us the postcode of an address she wants to meet us at.'

'And the 1130 at the end could be the time she wants to meet up,' said Sienna. 'Perhaps she wants to meet at that postcode at 11.30.'

Sophie opened the Google app on her phone and punched in the postcode. On the map, it turned out to be an address in Bermondsey on the south side of the River Thames.

'I think this might be it,' she said, 'and it's not that far. We can cross the river to Waterloo underground station and take the Jubilee Line out to Bermondsey.'

As they headed south over Waterloo Bridge, Sophie looked across the water to the apartment block that was the scene of yesterday's battle. Less than twenty-four hours ago she had been up on that roof, clinging to a rope and sliding perilously close to the edge. If she hadn't been able to brace herself against the parapet, she would have plummeted helplessly to the concrete down below. Her hands still bore the scratches from where she had clung onto the jagged pipe the rope was attached to, but it could have been so much worse.

After travelling underground for ten minutes, the girls emerged into the light at Bermondsey station then headed south towards the meeting point Nightfly had given them. The landscape here was very different from the scene they had left behind in central London. Light industrial space and warehouses rubbed shoulders with a few rudimentary shops and sprawling estates of high rise apartment blocks. Everything had a rough feeling about it. On this cold December day, it felt grey and slightly intimidating.

When they reached the area of the postcode, they paused for a moment and thought about where Nightfly might be waiting for them. It was mostly residential property but for a small row of shops that served the local people, including a launderette, a Chinese restaurant and a shabby looking hairdresser. There was also a shop that appeared to sell almost everything with a sign saying 'Open from 6.00 am until Midnight' plastered across the window. Several Christmas trees were leaning up against a wall outside the shop, and a woman wearing a battered overcoat and a pair of reindeer antlers was standing beside them scrolling through her phone. She didn't look at all Christmassy.

On the opposite side of the road was an old three-storey warehouse that looked as if it hadn't been used for years. The windows on the ground floor had all been boarded up, and there was a large crack running the length of the outside wall.

'Do you think that's it?' said Sophie as they surveyed the ramshackle building.

'I can't think where else it could be. Let's go and take a look.'

Sophie felt as if the eyes of the neighbourhood were on her as they crossed over to the other side of the road. She didn't belong on these streets, and she sensed that the people and even the buildings were aware of it. It was such a contrast to the quiet affluence of Hampton

Spa. She was an outsider here. She felt conspicuous and ill at ease. But she knew that it was important for her to stay calm as if what they were doing was just a normal part of her day. The last thing Sienna needed was the police to be called because two girls had broken into a vacant warehouse building.

Sienna tried the main door, expecting it to be firmly locked, and was surprised to find that it opened quite easily. Someone was obviously expecting them. They stepped inside and shut the door behind them. With the windows boarded up from the outside, it was difficult to see much in the pitch-black interior. Sophie took out her phone and switched on the flashlight. As she did, a text arrived. It read 'Second floor. No lights.' The girls were now sure they had found the right building.

Scanning the beam of light around the desolate interior, Sophie located the staircase then shut off the flashlight. It didn't take long for their eyes to become accustomed to the darkness. Soon they could make out enough vague shapes to be able to move cautiously across the floor towards the stairs.

'If this is Nightfly,' Sienna whispered, 'don't forget she has a gun. And that last night she tried to murder a man by strapping a bomb to him.'

On hearing Sienna's words, Sophie's mind started racing with all the possibilities of disaster. Why were they taking the risk of agreeing to meet Nightfly in such an isolated spot? She may have changed sides again and agreed to lure the girls into a trap. Perhaps Osorio or Jacobs had caught up with Nightfly and were now using Sienna's phone to ensnare them. Sophie thought about turning back, regrouping so they could get a dialogue started by text, but Sienna was already moving up the staircase.

There was a stale smell in the air, a smell of dust and rust and decay. In the distant past, this building might have been a thriving hub of industry; a place where men and women earned an honest living to support their families. But that time was long gone. Now it was an empty shell, echoing with the sound of the girls' tentative footsteps.

The stairs creaked and moaned as they carefully made their way upwards. At one point the staircase shuddered as if it might give way at any minute. Sophie grabbed hold of Sienna's arm to steady herself, unnerved by the prospect of crashing through the rotting timbers to the darkness down below. It was like walking on very thin ice.

When they reached the next floor, the light was not much better than it had been downstairs. The curtains had been drawn to block out the sun, and they could barely see more than a few feet in front of themselves. Sophie could feel the fear rising in her chest. If they had walked into a trap, it was too late to turn back now. They inched their way into the centre of the room. The silence was unnerving. The only noise the girls could hear was the sound of their own footsteps crunching across the debris that littered the floor.

'Hello,' Sienna shouted. 'Is anybody here?'

She was about to call out again when a bright light came on, a blinding light that was shining directly into their eyes. They put their hands up in front of their faces to protect themselves from the glare. As she squinted through her fingers, Sophie could just make out the silhouette of a girl. She was standing several feet in front of them. And she was holding a gun.

Had they walked into a trap? Should they have told Jutan where they were going? They should never have allowed themselves to be drawn into such a vulnerable position. It was a hopelessly naïve thing to do. Now they would have to face the consequences of their folly.

'Put your phone on the floor and back away from it,' said the girl's voice. Sienna recognised the voice instantly. It was Nightfly.

Chapter Fifteen

They stood perfectly still for a few seconds.

'The phone,' Nightfly demanded. 'Put it on the floor and move right away from it.'

Sophie put her phone on the ground, and the girls backed away to the wall at the far side. Once they were out of the glare of the light, they could just make out the figure of Nightfly bending down to pick up the phone.

'I'm checking your calls and texts to make sure you haven't told anyone that you're meeting me here,' she said.

A few seconds later, she seemed to be satisfied. She drew back the curtain, causing light to flood into the room. There was a silent tension between them for a few moments. Nightfly seemed unsure of what to say next. Finally, she walked over to where the girls were standing and handed the phone back to Sophie.

'So, you made it out of the warehouse alive then,' she said. She seemed ill at ease and still appeared to be on her guard.

'Yes, and so did Osorio,' Sienna answered. 'Sophie discovered where the timer was on the laptop, and she managed to stop the countdown.'

Nightfly looked surprised. 'Why would you want to save that snake's life? He'd happily have killed you and not given it a second thought.'

'He had something we wanted,' said Sophie. 'And besides, I couldn't just stand by and let you murder him.'

'So did you get what you were after?'

'We didn't get the chance,' said Sienna. 'Unfortunately, Jacobs and his driver arrived and we had to make a run for it.'

'You should have let him die,' said Nightfly, looking Sienna straight in the eye. 'Your sense of decency will kill you one day.'

They held each other's gaze for a few seconds, both of them still unsure whether they should let their guard down.

'What's with all the cryptic clues?' Sienna asked. 'You've got my phone. Why couldn't you have phoned us up instead of dragging us all the way over here?'

'I needed to find out whether I could trust you. I've been watching you from the window since you first arrived on the other side of the road. It doesn't look as if you're being followed, and now I've had the chance to check your phone records you don't appear to have contacted anyone since I texted you this morning.'

'So, what do you want?'

Nightfly paused for a moment, trying to think of the right words to say.

'I want you to get in touch with the Senate for me.'

'What makes you think I can contact the Senate?' said Sienna.

'You're a member of The Elite. You must have a line of command. I want you to broker a deal with them.'

'What kind of deal?'

Once again, Nightfly paused. She walked across to the window and stared down into the street.

'I want to go back to Galacdros,' she said. 'But before I decide whether to surrender myself, I'd like to find out what I'll be faced with.'

Sienna thought she looked haggard and tired as if she hadn't slept in some time. She had lost the swagger she displayed when they first met at the apartment the previous day. That girl would never have asked for anyone's help. So what had happened to bring about such an abrupt change?

'Why the sudden change of heart?' Sienna asked.

Nightfly looked out of the window at the cold December morning.

'It's time to stop fighting everyone. Now I know I'll never see my father again; I don't want to live like this anymore.'

On hearing the sadness in Nightfly's voice, Sophie couldn't help feeling a wave of sympathy for her. For so long, the thought of teaming up with her father again must have been the one thing that had driven her forward. She identified with him; they were kindred spirits. But when she found out she would never see him again, everything must have changed for her.

'I'm sorry you weren't able to find your father,' said Sophie. 'It must be a difficult thing to deal with after all these years.'

Nightfly didn't respond immediately. She seemed to be deep in thought.

'I was only seven when he was sent away,' she said, eventually, 'and I was too young to understand why he wasn't in his laboratory anymore. I kept thinking that one morning I'd wake up and he would be back at his desk, tinkering away with a circuit board. But he never was. So I buried myself in my computer. It was the only way I felt I could still have a part of him with me. And when I got older, I decided to take revenge on the people I blamed for sending him away.'

'Is that why you hacked into the computer at the Senate?' Sienna asked.

'Yes. I knew I could bypass their primitive security system, and I wanted to cause them as much pain and suffering as I could. I felt as if I was taking up arms against my father's enemies.'

They stood and talked for several minutes, and gradually a mutual trust began to develop between them. Nightfly seemed relieved to be able to unburden herself from the pain she had been carrying around inside. It was as if she could finally exhale after years of holding everything in.

'So, what do you think?' she said. 'Can you help me broker a deal?'

'There is someone I could call,' said Sienna. 'Her name is Jutan, and she has direct contact with the Senate.'

At the mention of Jutan's name, Sophie noticed Nightfly's eyes widen a little. It had been quite some time since Jutan left The Elite, but it was obvious that she was still held in very high esteem.

'Could we arrange a meeting with her?' Nightfly asked.

'I'll need my phone to do that,' said Sienna, reaching out her hand.

Nightfly hesitated for a moment then she reached into her pocket and handed over the phone. When Sienna made the call, it was a brief conversation. They arranged to meet in nearby Southwark Park. Jutan promised to come alone. Nightfly knew she was taking a massive risk, but there was no turning back now. She had made up her mind, and she was determined to keep moving forward.

Nothing much was said as they walked through the streets of South Bermondsey. When they reached the park gates there was no sign of Jutan. They made their way into the centre of the park to wait for her at the bandstand. In the cold light of day, Sophie thought Nightfly seemed noticeably smaller, almost fragile. Her mask of belligerence had slipped. She appeared vulnerable and filled with apprehension.

'Your father missed you very much,' said Sophie, as they waited for Jutan to appear. 'And he was desperate to get back to Galacdros to apologise for the pain he put your family through.'

Nightfly didn't respond. She took a deep breath and looked away. The emotion was starting to well up inside her. After a few seconds, she managed to compose herself and turn back towards Sophie.

'Where did you meet him?' she asked.

'On the outskirts of Hampton Spa; the town I live in. Osorio was holding us captive in some tunnels under your father's house and, when he made it clear he intended to kill us, your father helped us to escape. The three of us were chased by the guards, and eventually one of them shot your father. I'm afraid he died a few minutes later. We did what we could for him, but it was too late.'

Nightfly stared at the ground, thinking about what Sophie had said.

'But why did my father team up with a man like Osorio in the first place?'

'He thought it would give him the chance to return to Galacdros,' said Sienna.

'He was a good man,' Sophie added. 'He realised he had made a mistake, and he risked his life to fight against something that he believed to be unjust. I will always be grateful to him.'

A car pulled up outside the gates of the park, and seconds later they spotted Jutan striding along the path in their direction. Nightfly was immediately on edge, scanning the surrounding area for signs that she may not have come alone, but there wasn't another soul in the park. Jutan could obviously be taken at her word.

'Good afternoon, ladies,' said Jutan, as she joined them at the bandstand. 'And you must be Alicia Felso. I appreciate you trusting me to come alone, and I assure you I will not betray that trust.'

Nightfly reached out and shook Jutan's hand.

'Thank you for agreeing to meet me,' she said. 'I have a laptop in my bag that contains the plans that Osorio stole from the Ministry of Defence. It's the only copy he had, and I'm happy to hand it over to you as a token of goodwill.'

'And what are you looking for in return?' Jutan asked.

'I'd like your help in negotiating with the authorities in Galacdros. I know I'll have to go back and face justice sooner or later, but I'd rather do it on negotiated terms.'

'I'll do whatever I can to help,' said Jutan. 'And I applaud your decision to deal with this before it's too late.'

'Do you know where Osorio is now?' Sienna asked.

'I'm afraid I don't,' Nightfly answered. 'The only places I ever met with him were the apartment on the South Bank and on a houseboat.'

'A houseboat?' said Sienna. 'Where is this houseboat?'

'I don't know this city very well, so I couldn't tell you. But I remember there was a big bridge a little further down that could open up to let the ships pass through.'

'Tower Bridge,' said Sophie. 'It must be moored near Tower Bridge.'

'The houseboat is blue and white,' said Nightfly, 'and I think it's moored at a place called Raven's Wharf. I couldn't say whether he's there at the moment, but that's where I first met him.'

Sophie could tell that Sienna's mood had been lifted enormously by hearing this news. She had a new lead. The hunt was back on.

'There's one other thing I still don't understand,' said Sienna. 'What does Harry Jacobs have to do with all this? And why had he arranged to meet Osorio at the warehouse last night?'

'Osorio promised to let him make a copy of the plans we had stolen.'

Sienna looked across at Jutan, her eyes widening in shock.

'You don't think he intended to sell the plans to the Russians, do you? We saw a letter in his office yesterday that said he has massive gambling debts. This may have been his way to pay them all off.'

'Well that would explain why a suitcase changed hands at your hotel the other night,' said Jutan. 'And if that is the reason, Mr Jacobs will have been paid for something that he is now unable to deliver.'

There was plenty more that needed to be discussed, but Jutan didn't want to do it in such a public place. She turned to Nightfly.

'I think we should get you right away from here. I'm sure Osorio and Harry Jacobs will be desperate to get their hands on you, so we must find you a safe house then I will do what I can to negotiate your return to Galacdros.'

Jutan's driver was waiting for them at the gates of the park. He drove them back towards central London and dropped Sophie and Sienna outside London Bridge station. Just before the car pulled away, Jutan wound down the window and called the girls over.

'Keep a lookout for Mr Jacobs as you are travelling around the city,' she said. 'If our suspicions are correct and he intended to sell those plans to the Russians, he could now be a very desperate man. He will be well aware that his life is in great danger, and he will stop at nothing to get what he needs to survive.'

Chapter Sixteen

It was a short walk from London Bridge station to the hustle-bustle of Borough Market on the south side of the river. They sat in a coffee shop on the outer fringes of the market, eating lunch and discussing what their next move should be. Sienna only had one thing on her mind. The houseboat Nightfly had spoken of. She was determined to find it and establish whether Osorio was hiding out there.

'How far is it to Tower Bridge?' she asked.

'Not that far. We could probably walk there in about fifteen minutes.'

In the hubbub of the boisterous market, the girls had to speak up quite a bit to make themselves heard. It was a bustling festive atmosphere. On another day, Sophie would have happily spent several hours there, enjoying the delights that the market had to offer. But today there were more pressing things on her mind.

Sienna seemed very focussed, almost as if she knew that the final battle was about to occur. It had been five months since she first arrived in Sophie's world. If Osorio was on that houseboat, this could be the best chance she would ever get to recover The Orb. The two remaining guards will almost certainly have perished when they jumped into the river, so there was a fair chance that Osorio would be on his own.

Sophie took out her phone and thumbed the words 'Raven's Wharf' into Google.

'It's not coming up with much,' she said, looking at the results. 'Apparently, it's a small mooring near St Katharine Docks.'

Sienna narrowed her eyes and looked into the middle distance.

'OK,' she said, 'let's get over there and check it out.'

They finished their coffee and headed east down Tooley Street. Despite the cold weather, hoards of office workers were milling around, looking to get the most out of their lunch break. Sienna didn't say much as they headed towards the docks. There was a determined look in her eyes. She was clearly in battle mode.

As they passed a busy sandwich shop, a car pulled up

next to them. The driver was wearing a baseball cap and a pair of sunglasses. He held out a copy of the local street map to ask Sophie for directions. By the time she realised who he was, it was too late. It was Harry Jacobs' driver, and under the map she could see that he was pointing a gun at her.

'Get in the back, both of you!' he grunted. 'I'm quite happy to use this gun in broad daylight.'

He sounded unhinged, and Sophie was convinced he was mad enough to do it. When they opened the door and climbed into the back seat, they were immediately confronted with Harry Jacobs. He looked agitated and dishevelled, and Sophie was sure that the hand inside his coat was holding a gun. As the car pulled away, Jacobs stuck the barrel of the gun into Sophie's ribs. It was a stark warning that he meant business. They travelled in silence for a few minutes. Finally, they reached a secluded side street next to a rundown piece of parkland.

'I want to know where that girl is,' said Jacobs, glaring at the girls.

'We don't know,' said Sienna. 'We're looking for her as well.'

'Don't lie to me,' Jacobs spat back at her. 'If you don't tell me where she is I'll gladly dispose of both of you right here and now. Your interfering has cost me everything I've worked for, and I'll happily dump your bodies here in the street.'

He looked like a man who hadn't slept in a week. He was unshaven and his clothes were unkempt, a stark contrast to the Harry Jacobs Sophie was used to seeing on TV. A twitch on the left-hand side of his face was making him squint slightly in one eye. Sophie just stared at him in terror. She was so frozen with fear that she could barely breathe.

'We're not lying,' she pleaded. 'We honestly don't know where she is.'

Jacobs was clearly a desperate man. Heavily in debt, his reputation and political career in tatters, he looked so unbalanced that Sophie was convinced she was about to die.

'You!' Jacobs barked, looking across at Sienna. 'Tell me where that girl is or you'll be saying goodbye to your friend.' He lifted the gun and pointed it at Sophie's head.

Sienna hesitated for a second. She couldn't risk making a grab for the gun. The surprise might make it go off. But she knew she had to do something.

'Last chance!' Jacobs shouted. He had become

hysterical and he sounded totally deranged.

Just then, a middle-aged lady appeared on the street corner not far from where their car was parked. She was walking a small dog on a lead, and they appeared to be on their way to the parkland on the other side of the road. On seeing her, Jacobs gritted his teeth and slipped the gun back inside his jacket. The twitch on the side of his face became more pronounced, and he clenched his fist in frustration. He hadn't expected to be disturbed like this. Now he would have to bide his time and wait for the woman and her dog to pass by.

The woman was moving very slowly, allowing the dog to sniff around whenever it found something of interest. Sophie thought she looked like a kind lady, mild-mannered and understated. She was very elegantly dressed, and she seemed quite content to let her little dog take its time as it nuzzled at whatever it could find on the ground. For a few seconds, Sophie thought about appealing to her for help. In the end she decided against it. Why drag this poor innocent woman into trouble?

When they reached the side of the car, the dog sniffed around at the front wheel for a moment then raised its leg and relieved itself. The driver smiled at the woman, hoping she wouldn't sense the tension that was palpable inside the car. She smiled politely back at him then took a small handgun from inside her coat and shot him point blank through the head. Before anyone could react, she turned the gun on Jacobs and dealt with him in the same ruthless fashion.

Now that Sophie could see her close up, she was acutely aware of the cold look in her eyes. But the woman took no account of the girls at all. It was as if they didn't exist. A car screeched to a halt a few feet further down the road, and the woman picked up the dog, muttered something affectionate to it in Russian and climbed into the back seat. Within seconds they were gone, and the girls were left to deal with the carnage she had created.

'We've got to get out of here,' said Sienna, pushing the door of the car open.

Sophie was in shock. The suddenness and brutality of the attack had left her feeling totally numb. Two lives had been snuffed out with ruthless efficiency right in front of her. She was finding it hard to speak.

'Sophie, let's go!' Sienna shouted, pulling at her arm. 'We can't be anywhere near here when they find these bodies.'

She dragged Sophie out of the car and back up the street, keen to get as far away from the scene of the crime as possible. But it was slow going. The clinical nature of the attack had been such a shock that Sophie was finding it hard to think straight.

As soon as they reached the main road, Sienna contacted Jutan to tell her what had happened. She knew it was vital that British security agents reached the scene of the murder before the police did, and Jutan would want to inform them straight away. If news ever leaked out that the British Home Secretary had betrayed his country to the Russians, and paid the ultimate price, it would be a major embarrassment for the country.

Despite Sophie's distress, Sienna was keen to continue the hunt for Osorio. If the Russians had murdered Harry Jacobs, they must be desperate to get their hands on those plans, and they may believe they are still in Osorio's possession. There was no time to waste. She had to get to him before the Russians did, or her chance of recovering The Orb may be lost forever.

They pressed on towards the river. Sophie was still in shock. The execution of Jacobs and his driver had been so out of the blue that she was now starkly aware of her own mortality. A feeling of insecurity and fear was beginning to overwhelm her. She didn't know whether she could carry on.

When they reached the bank of the River Thames, they made their way along the riverside walkway to Butler's Wharf. Sienna looked across to the north side of the river. She could see St Katharine Docks and the vast array of vessels rubbing shoulders with the restaurants and cafes that surrounded them. And further down were the more exposed moorings of Raven's Wharf, where a small selection of houseboats were bobbing about on the open river.

'Well, if that's where the houseboat is,' said Sienna, 'he'd definitely have a good view of Tower Bridge.'

Sophie didn't respond. It was becoming harder and harder to keep going. She wanted to stand by her friend and help her in her quest, but the brutality of what she had just witnessed was starting to take its toll on her. She felt lost and hopelessly out of her depth.

'Let's cross the river and take a closer look,' said Sienna. 'We're almost there now. This could be the moment we've been waiting for.'

Walking over Tower Bridge, Sienna couldn't take her eyes off the collection of houseboats that were moored just a little further down. She seemed unaware of the emotional turmoil that had taken hold of Sophie. These were battle conditions, and Sienna only had one thing on her mind. She had waited so long for this chance. If Osorio was holed up on one of those houseboats, she was determined to make this opportunity count.

At the other side of the bridge, they made their way down the stone steps onto the Thames path and headed east looking for Raven's Wharf. It was a cold day, and the stiff breeze that was blowing in off the river made it feel a good deal colder. Sophie pulled the collar of her jacket up around her neck and looked across at Sienna. There was an intense look in her eyes. She was like a hound on the scent of its prey, caught up in the frenzy of the hunt, rushing headlong towards the kill. Sophie was worried that she wasn't thinking straight and might end up taking too big a risk. She had to make sure Sienna didn't do anything reckless.

When they were only about forty metres from Raven's Wharf, Sienna stopped suddenly and pulled Sophie into a doorway.

'There he is,' she said, in an excited whisper.

Sophie looked at the houseboats but couldn't see Osorio anywhere.

'There,' said Sienna, 'the white boat with the blue roof.'

When Sophie looked again, she could just make out

Osorio moving around inside the boat. They had found him, and he appeared to be on his own. So what did Sienna plan to do next? There was plenty of cover along the path; doorways that could be ducked into. It would be easy to keep an eye on Osorio until they could summon Jutan and her agents. But Sophie knew that Sienna wouldn't be prepared to wait. The time for waiting was over. This was her moment. This was her destiny.

Chapter Seventeen

'He seems to be on his own,' said Sienna. 'If I can take him by surprise, he may not have time to react.'

'Shouldn't we wait for Jutan?' Sophie asked with an increasing sense of alarm.

'I've been waiting five months for this chance. I'm not waiting around any longer.'

Sienna took out her phone and thumbed in a text to Jutan, telling her they had found Osorio and giving her the exact location. Then she switched the phone off and slipped it into her back pocket. Sophie knew that Jutan would want the girls to wait until she arrived, but Sienna was already planning her attack.

'Maybe I should swim to the other side of the boat and strike from there. It will be the last thing he'll be expecting.'

'Sienna, don't,' Sophie pleaded. 'There are dangerous

currents and undertows in this part of the river that can drag you under in seconds. Even strong swimmers shouldn't be swimming anywhere around here.'

Sienna thought for a moment.

'OK,' she said. 'It looks like I'll have to go in through the front door.'

Despite the horrific events she had already witnessed that day, Sophie knew she couldn't let Sienna do this alone.

'And I'm going in with you,' she said.

'No, Sophie, you can't. We need someone to be here when Jutan arrives. If anything goes wrong, we have to make sure Osorio doesn't manage to get away.'

'But what if he's not alone? You could be walking into a trap.'

'Whatever fate has to throw at me, I'm ready for it,' said Sienna. 'I can't just hide back here and wait for exactly the right moment to attack. That's not who I am. I'm going in.'

She stepped forward to the edge of the doorway and prepared to advance on the houseboat.

'Sienna, wait,' said Sophie, reaching forward and grabbing her by the arm. But when Sienna turned around, Sophie was suddenly lost for words. There was so much that she wanted to say, so much she wanted to tell Sienna about their friendship and how much it meant to her, but her mind seemed to completely seize up. Finally, she just looked into her eyes and smiled.

'Take care,' she said.

Sienna leaned forward and gave her a hug. Then she darted out of the doorway and ran down the path towards the houseboat. It was a tense few seconds. She was very exposed, and Osorio could have turned and spotted her at any moment. But she managed to get quite close to the mooring before ducking behind a pillar to gather her thoughts.

Osorio appeared to be talking to someone on the telephone. He was pacing up and down the cabin, gesticulating wildly and shouting aggressively into the phone. There seemed to be a pattern to his pacing. Up to the front of the boat, pause, talk for a few moments, then back to the other end of the boat. If he continued to repeat this pattern, Sienna calculated that she would have thirteen seconds when he had his back to the entrance to the cabin.

When he turned and started walking away from her again, she rushed across the road and carefully stepped onto the boat. The door to the cabin was slightly open. It creaked a little as she inched her way inside. Thankfully, Osorio was shouting so much that he was unaware of the noise.

This was the moment Sienna had been waiting for. There were no armed guards or androids to contend with, and something in her heart told her there was nobody else on the boat. This time it was one against one, and Sienna was determined to emerge from the battle victorious.

As Osorio turned to walk back towards the front of the boat, he was so engrossed in his conversation that he only had a split second before Sienna smashed into him and knocked him forcefully to the ground. They rolled on the floor of the houseboat, trading kicks and punches, each trying to gain the upper hand.

All the pent up emotion of the last five months seemed to pour out of Sienna. Osorio may have been bigger and more powerful than her, but her relentless onslaught gradually started to unnerve him. He scrambled to his feet and pulled a handgun from inside his jacket. Sienna's reaction was instinctive. She pivoted on the heel of her palm and lashed out with her foot, just managing to kick the gun out of his hand. It flew through the air and clattered to the floor, scudding across the floorboards and ending up under a wooden storage cupboard in the far corner.

Now it was down to hand-to-hand combat. Osorio was tall and strong and ought to have had an advantage, but Sienna was possessed by a primitive power that drove her forward in her hunger to retake The Orb. For once Osorio seemed a little hesitant as if he knew he was up against some sort of mighty force. His usual arrogance had deserted him, and the longer the fight went on the more he seemed to be on the defensive.

He grabbed hold of a table lamp, ripping the cord from the wall, and started brandishing it as a makeshift weapon. Sienna advanced. Osorio swung the lamp, but she ducked under it and caught him on the side of the head with a well-aimed punch. He reeled back in surprise, continuing to brandish the table lamp defensively. It didn't stop Sienna's advance.

'Give me The Orb,' she shouted, a ferocious desire burning inside her heart. 'Your time is up Osorio; I'm not leaving here without The Orb.'

Stepping forward as if she was about to attack, she waited for Osorio to swing the lamp again. This time she dodged to the side then caught him square in the chest with a savage heel kick. He gasped in pain as it knocked him backwards, sending him clattering into the wall.

Osorio was now becoming quite alarmed. Backing away from Sienna's furious assault, he flung the lamp at her in a desperate attempt to halt her forward progress. It took her completely by surprise. She threw up her arm to try to deflect the lamp, but it smacked into the side of her head, causing her to stumble momentarily and slump down onto her knees. Osorio knew that he had to grasp this moment.

Rushing over to where the gun had scudded under the cupboard, he pushed his arm underneath and began furiously hunting for the missing weapon. It was a frantic search. He groped around for several seconds before his fingertips finally touched something metal. If he could just get a firm grip on it, he could finish this matter now. Gradually he managed to get more of his fingers onto the gun, and he carefully began pulling it out.

But before he could get the gun into his hand, a pair of boots crunched down onto his arm, and the searing pain made him pull back and roll out of the way. Sienna was back on her feet, and she looked a nightmarish sight. There was a crazed look in her eyes. Blood had matted her hair to one side of her head, and her clothes were bloodied and torn. She was a force of nature and Osorio was now beginning to worry that she was unstoppable.

He grabbed a knife from one of the cupboard drawers and held it out in front of himself in an effort to keep her at bay. Osorio was now operating out of fear. Sienna was being driven forward by a primal spirit, intent on victory at all costs.

As she continued to advance, he flung the knife at her in desperation. It zipped past her ear, missing her by millimetres. Unable to think of another way to stop her, Osorio turned and ran towards the door. But as he bolted out through the cabin door, Sienna caught up with him, and suddenly they were wrestling on the side of the boat.

Osorio was now in a total panic. For once in his life he was the hunted party, and his actions were becoming more and more frantic. He tried to get his hands around Sienna's throat, anything to slow down her onslaught, and in their furious struggle to overpower one another, they both overbalanced and plunged into the freezing water of the river.

Sophie gasped with horror when she saw Sienna disappearing under the water. She sprinted across the road and leapt onto the small pier that led to where the houseboat was berthed. Sienna and Osorio were thrashing about in the river. The savage cold of the water was sapping their strength, but still they continued to fight at close quarters.

Osorio landed a heavy blow to the side of Sienna's head. Seconds later they both ducked under the water again. Sophie knew she couldn't stay on the sidelines any longer. She ripped off her jacket, intent on jumping in to rescue Sienna, but at the last minute she heard the sound of someone calling her name.

'I told her to wait until I arrived,' said Jutan, rushing up to where Sophie stood. 'How long have they been in the water?'

'About a minute or so,' said Sophie.

'We have to get her out of there. In these temperatures, the freezing water will kill her.'

Osorio's head appeared above the water once more. This time he was on his own. Seconds later Sienna reappeared, spluttering and gasping for air. On seeing her, Osorio's eyes widened with fear, and he started to swim out into the open river. Sienna didn't waste any time in giving chase.

'This is madness,' said Jutan. 'The currents out there are treacherous.'

She scanned the surrounding area. At the end of the pier, there was a small rowboat tethered to a post. It didn't have an outboard motor, but there were two oars lying across the seats.

'Let's take that boat,' she said. 'We've got to get Sienna out of there.'

They leapt into the boat, took one oar each and hauled themselves out into the open river. When she turned her head, Sophie could see Sienna and Osorio wrestling in the water but now the fight was less intense. They both appeared to be struggling to stay afloat, and it wasn't long before they slipped under again.

'Sienna!' Sophie shouted, looking intently at the spot where they had disappeared. She slipped off her boots and stood up. 'She needs our help. I have to go in and find her.'

'I can't let you do it,' said Jutan, pulling her back down into the boat. 'You'll be in just as much danger as she is. The next time she surfaces, we'll grab hold of her arms and drag her out of the water.'

They sat and watched the murky river, hoping desperately for a sighting of Sienna. Sophie kept expecting her to burst to the surface at any moment and take a massive lungful of air, but the time ticked by and there was no sign of her anywhere. It was a tortuous, despairing wait. Sophie could barely breathe. As more time passed, and there was still no sign of Sienna, she stared at the Thames in disbelief.

'She's been under for quite a while now,' said Jutan, an air of sadness in her voice. 'It's hard to believe that anyone could survive for this long.'

'No!' Sophie shouted. 'She's still OK; I know she is.' But despite her bravado, she was shouting out of hope rather than belief.

The only sound they could hear was the water lapping against the side of the boat. Jutan put a hand on Sophie's shoulder.

'I'm so sorry, Sophie,' she said. 'I'm afraid she may have been taken by the current.'

The shock of hearing Jutan's words was too much for Sophie. She collapsed onto the floor of the boat, and her emotions came flooding out.

'Why didn't she wait for you?' she said, between sobs. 'There was no need for her to rush in. This is all my fault; I should have stopped her.'

'There was nothing you could have said that would have persuaded her to wait,' said Jutan. 'She was passionate and principled and determined to complete her mission.'

Sophie turned and stared in disbelief at the spot where Sienna had been taken. The silent power of the river had swallowed her up.

Chapter Eighteen

Sophie refused to believe that it was over. It couldn't be. She had always believed Sienna to be invincible, so strong and powerful that not even the mighty River Thames could defeat her. She sat in the little rowboat, looking for any sign that a miracle could occur, hoping Sienna hadn't given up the fight.

'Please don't go, Sienna,' she whispered, tears creeping down her face.

The water looked dark and unforgiving. Somewhere down there Sienna could be fighting for her life, struggling against the currents and undertows that make this part of the river so dangerous. She had such a formidable spirit. Surely, even now, there was a chance that she would overcome the odds.

They sat and waited, watching and listening for any signs of life. The river was strangely silent and still as if it too was mourning the loss of Sienna. Everything was melancholy and grey. All the colour had been drained out of the world, and Sophie felt like everything was draining out of her too. There would be a massive hole in her life without Sienna.

The silence was suddenly shattered when a commotion of noise came from close by, and Sophie's eyes widened in shock when she saw Sienna, bedraggled and battered, gasping for air and clinging to the rope that was trailing from the back of the boat.

'Sienna!' she shouted, lurching forward and dragging her friend towards her.

They hauled her out of the water into the relative warmth of the rowboat. She was shivering and unable to speak, and her eyes were barely open. But she was alive and that was all that mattered. As she lay on the floor of the boat, shaking uncontrollably, Jutan took her coat off and wrapped it around Sienna's frozen body. Then they rowed back towards the pier as quickly as they could, carried her onto the houseboat and laid her down on the sofa.

Sophie rushed into the bedroom, grabbed the duvet off the bed and draped it over Sienna in an effort to warm her up.

'We have to get her to a doctor,' she said. 'She's been in that freezing water much too long.'

'We can't take her to a regular doctor,' said Jutan, 'but I'll contact someone in British Intelligence and get her into a military hospital.'

After a few minutes, Sienna opened her eyes a little. When she saw Sophie and Jutan, the hint of a smile flickered across her face. She coughed, but the effort took so much out of her that she winced and closed her eyes again.

'It's OK, Sienna,' said Sophie. 'We've got help coming. We're going to get you to a doctor.'

Sienna was too weak to protest, but not too weak to celebrate. Using what little strength she had left, she raised her limp arm from under the duvet and opened up her clenched fist. Displayed on her outstretched palm was a small smooth stone the size of a walnut. Somehow she had managed to take The Orb from Osorio, and somehow she had managed to survive the cold and currents of the mighty River Thames. Against all the odds, Sienna's indomitable spirit had triumphed at last.

They heard the sound of a powerboat pulling alongside the pier. Seconds later, Jutan's phone rang to announce that the medics had arrived to take Sienna to a military hospital.

'How long was she in the water for?' the paramedic asked.

'I'm not sure,' said Sophie, 'about fifteen minutes or so.'

The paramedic looked shocked.

'It's a miracle she's still alive,' she said. 'This young lady must have a very powerful life force.'

'She certainly does,' said Jutan. 'She is a remarkable young woman.'

They wrapped Sienna in a warm blanket, then Sophie and Jutan followed on behind as the paramedics carried her out to the powerboat. Further down the river, they were transferred to a helicopter, and soon they were touching down on the roof of a small hospital in central London.

It would be a while before Sienna was strong enough to talk about what had happened. The doctors wanted her to sleep as much as possible, and as the day wore on Sophie and Jutan were advised to come back the following morning.

As she sat having dinner with her mum later that evening, Sophie felt uncomfortable trying to explain why Sienna wasn't there.

'She had a call from an old friend of her father's,' she said, trying to stay as close to the truth as possible. 'She's visiting London for a few days, and Sienna wanted to meet up with her.'

'Oh really,' said Mrs Watson. 'And did you get to meet her?'

'Yes, I did,' Sophie answered, 'and I'm not surprised Sienna was keen to spend some time with her.'

The following morning Mrs Watson had an 8:00 a.m. meeting in the city, so Sophie ended up eating breakfast on her own. As she stared out of the window onto The Strand, she wondered if this was how it would be for her from now on. For the last two months she had enjoyed eating breakfast with Sienna every morning, but now The Orb had been recovered she was sure Sienna would want to return home to Galacdros. And even though she was excited for her friend, it would be a difficult moment when she finally had to say goodbye.

Crossing the lobby on her way back up to her room, she passed a table displaying a range of complimentary magazines and newspapers. When she saw the story that was on the front page of every paper, it stopped her dead in her tracks.

'Harry Jacobs dies in horrific car crash,' said one headline. 'Home Secretary killed in tragic car accident,' said another.

According to the newspapers, the car skidded off the road in a remote area of rural Kent, crashing into a tree and killing him instantly. The Intelligence Service had done a great job on the cover-up. All the papers carried glowing tributes to a man who they claimed had 'served his country with distinction.' Sophie stared at the headlines for a few moments, wondering whether she could ever believe what was printed in the newspapers again.

She was awoken from her thoughts when the hotel door swung open, and Jutan appeared in the doorway. When she saw Sophie looking at the headlines, she frowned and walked across the lobby to join her.

'Ah yes,' said Jutan, picking up one of the newspapers. 'I know it makes for uncomfortable reading, but I think Mr Jacobs' family have enough to deal with right now without being forced to face the truth.'

'Have you seen Sienna?' Sophie asked.

'Yes, I have,' Jutan answered, smiling broadly. 'I've just come from the hospital and Sienna appears to have had a very good night.'

Sophie breathed a sigh of relief. 'So she's going to be OK then?'

'The doctor is confident she will make a full recovery.

In fact, that's why I'm here. Sienna asked if you could take her a change of clothes. She's been told that she can leave the hospital as soon as she's ready.'

It was a brisk walk through the streets of London to the small hospital where Sienna was staying. Jutan set quite a fast pace and Sophie had to work hard to keep up.

'What do you think Sienna will do now?' Sophie asked as they approached the hospital.

'That's entirely up to her,' Jutan answered, 'but I'm sure she will want to return to Galacdros with The Orb. It was an extraordinary act of heroism on her part to take on this mission, and she deserves to bask in the glory of her achievement. As for the future, who knows what she will do?'

It was an emotional moment for Sophie when she first saw Sienna. The colour had returned to her face and she looked vibrant and upbeat, but there were several stitches in a shaved area at the side of her head and her upper lip was cut and badly bruised. She looked like a war survivor, which wasn't that far from the truth.

Jutan reached into the pocket of her coat, took out a small silk purse and handed it to Sienna. Inside was The Orb she had fought so hard to retrieve.

'How many people have died because of this small stone?' Sienna asked. 'It really is a powerful force in the wrong hands.'

'But if it wasn't for this stone, we may never have met,' said Sophie, 'so maybe it also has the power to do good.'

Sienna nodded and smiled, then reached across to give her friend a hug.

'And what a powerful combination you two have become,' said Jutan. 'To defeat a man like Osorio is quite an achievement. You should both be very proud of yourselves.'

'What happened to Osorio?' Sienna asked.

'There has been no sign of him anywhere,' said Jutan. 'My best guess is that he perished under the water and his body may wash up further down the estuary. But I have learned over the years to take nothing for granted. Until we have a definite sighting of him he is officially still at large. So we must all be on our guard.'

When they stepped out into the crisp December air, Sienna was still a little unsteady on her feet. Jutan and Sophie walked one on either side of her while they made their way back across London to the Imperial Hotel. But despite her unsteadiness, nothing could dampen the euphoria Sienna was feeling. She had completed her first mission for The Elite, and a heavy weight of expectation had been lifted from her shoulders.

'The news of your success has been very well received in Galacdros,' said Jutan, as they dodged through the tourists and Christmas shoppers swarming around in London's West End. 'And your father is very proud that you are about to return home with The Orb.'

'I've been waiting for this moment for a very long time,' said Sienna.

'Well, you won't have to wait much longer. I have arranged for a car to take us down to Dorset later today so we can travel through the portal back to our world. And I will accompany you to make sure there are no problems.'

Sophie bit her lip and tried to stop the sadness from overwhelming her. She was aware what a great day it would be for Sienna when she returned to Galacdros. But what did it mean for their friendship? They had been through so much together in the last five months. Was this the last time they would ever see one another?

Back at the hotel, Sienna gathered all her things together and packed them into her bag. It was the same backpack she was wearing when she first burst into Sophie's life five action-packed months ago. They sat in the bistro having coffee and cake, laughing together and reminding one another of some of the more comical events they had been through. Sophie tried hard not to think about Sienna's imminent departure.

'When you think you're ready for action again,' said Jutan, 'I'm sure The Elite will be proud to have you back in their team. But there's something else I would like you to consider. I could use someone here in my team who has good instincts and is used to working in this world. I've been given permission by the Senate to offer you a position as one of my agents.'

Sienna nodded, trying to take in what Jutan had just offered her.

'You don't have to give me your decision straight away, but promise me that you'll think about it.'

'What do you think?' said Sophie, trying to keep her excitement under control.

'I don't know,' Sienna answered. 'This is all a bit sudden. I don't really know what to say.'

'Once you've had a chance to gain closure on this mission, I think you'll find it easy to answer that question,' said Jutan. 'For now, enjoy your moment of triumph and know there's always a position for you here in this world.'

'And a friend who will be very glad to see you again,' said Sophie.

'Don't worry,' said Sienna, smiling back at her, 'you haven't seen the last of me.'

When it was time for Sienna to leave, Sophie stood on the front steps of the hotel and waved as the car pulled away into the traffic. It was difficult to hold back the tears. Meeting Sienna had been such a transformational experience for her that Sophie couldn't imagine what it would be like to not have her around. But the girl that Sienna had left behind was not the same cautious, risk-averse person she met all those months ago. She was strong and confident and ready to take on whatever life had to throw at her.

She watched and waved until the car was no longer visible at the far end of The Strand. Then she went up to her room, collapsed onto the bed and surrendered to her grief.

She had been asleep for some time when there was a knock at her door. On opening it, she was greeted by the smiling face of her dad.

'Sorry darling, were you asleep?' he asked. 'Only you'd better get a move on if we're going to get to Downing Street by three-thirty.'

Sophie looked at her watch. She hadn't intended to sleep for so long, and they were expected in Downing Street in just over an hour. Mr Watson looked past her into the room with a puzzled look on his face.

'Where's Sienna?' he asked. 'Should I give her a call?'

'Erm, no,' said Sophie. 'Sienna won't be coming with us. She had a call from her dad. She's had to go back home for a while.'

'Nothing serious, I hope,' said Mr Watson.

'Oh no,' Sophie answered. 'It's some sort of celebration. But it's just going to be you, me and Mum who'll be going to Downing Street.'

It was a proud moment for Sophie when she set off for Downing Street with her mum and dad. The Prime Minister had sent a car for them, and they attracted a small crowd as they climbed into the back just outside the Imperial Hotel.

As the car drove through the security gates of Downing Street, Sophie thought about Sienna's triumphant return to Galacdros. She knew how much it meant to Sienna to be able to step out of her father's shadow and be a revered member of the community in her own right. And even though she would miss her friend terribly, it was great to know that Sienna would always be celebrated as the agent who had returned The Orb to the Senate.

Tea with the Prime Minister was a more relaxed affair than she had expected. Away from the cameras and microphones, she thought he was a decent man with a good sense of humour. And he seemed genuinely grateful that Sophie had risked her life to foil Osorio's attempt to assassinate him when he visited Hampton Spa.

'So what have you been up to while you've been here in London?' the Prime Minister asked.

'Oh, the usual stuff,' said Sophie. 'You know, shopping and seeing the sights, basically just hanging out with my best friend.'

'So no heroics or hunting down assassins then?' said the Prime Minister, smiling broadly.

'Do I look like the sort of person who would go looking for trouble?' Sophie said, smiling back at him.

Maybe she imagined it, but as she spoke the words, she was sure she could hear the sound of Sienna's laughter.

If you enjoyed this book…

Thank you so much for checking out Sophie and Sienna's latest adventure.

If you enjoyed reading the book, I'd be very grateful if you could spend a minute leaving a review on the book's Amazon page. Even one short sentence would be very much appreciated.

Reviews make a real difference to authors. They help other readers get a feel for the book, and I would also be very interested to hear your thoughts on the story.

Thank you for your help,

A.B. Martin

Acknowledgements

Many thanks to Dane at ebooklaunch.com for the stunning cover design. And a very big thank you to my wife, Annie Burchell, without whose help this book would still be a work in progress. Her inspirational ideas and thoughtful and detailed advice really helped me to get the best out of this story.

About the author

A.B. Martin is an English author who writes thrilling middle-grade adventure stories and intriguing mysteries.

Before becoming an author, he wrote extensively for television and radio and performed comedy in a vast array of venues, including the world-famous London Palladium.

Raven's Wharf is the third book in the Sophie Watson Adventure Mystery series. It was published in November 2019.

He lives in London, England, with his wife and daughter.

Also by A.B. Martin

Kestrel Island

In a sleepy English seaside town, Sophie Watson is enjoying a peaceful holiday in the sunshine. But when she befriends a mysterious and charismatic girl called Sienna, she is drawn into a heart-stopping adventure where the future security of the world may be under threat.

To find out the truth, they must go to Kestrel Island. The plot they uncover is more mind-blowing than they could possibly have imagined.

Can Sophie find the courage she needs to survive? Or will the secret the girls uncover put them in mortal danger?

One thing is certain: Sophie's life is about to change forever.

Also by A.B. Martin
Under Crook's Wood

A strange creature has been spotted in Crook's Wood on the outskirts of Hampton Spa. Was it just a trick of the light, or is there something more sinister and dangerous going on? There's certainly something odd about Heath Grange, the mysterious ramshackle house on the edge of the wood.

When Sophie and Sienna decide to investigate, they might be walking into a trap. An enemy from the past is watching their every move, and their lives could be in mortal danger.

Will their first reunion be their last?

Printed in Great Britain
by Amazon